D1809707

NIL BY MOUTH

LynC

SHOOTING STAR

SHOOTING STAR PRESS

First published in Australia in 2019
by Shooting Star Press
PO Box 6813, Charnwood ACT 2615
info@shootingstar.pub
www.shootingstar.pub

ABN 63 158 506 524

This collection copyright © LynC 2019

The right of LynC to be identified as the author of this work has
been asserted by them in accordance with the *Copyright Amendment
(Moral Rights) Act 2000*. All rights reserved.

Other than brief extracts, no part of this publication may be
produced in any form without the written consent of the
Publisher. The Publisher makes no representation or warranty
regarding the accuracy, timeliness, suitability or any other aspect
of the information contained in this book and cannot accept any
legal responsibility or liability for any errors or omissions that may
be made.

A catalogue record for this book is available from the National
Library of Australia.

C, Lyn.
    Nil by Mouth
    ISBN: 978-1-925821-21-5   PRINT
    ISBN: 978-1-925821-22-2   EBOOK

Edited by Serena Sandrin
Cover models & photography by Lewis
Typesetting by Debbie Phillips, DP Plus

The rain felt wonderful on my face and in my eyes. After months, or was it years, stuck in a windowless room, unable to even move, just lying here on the cold hard ground in the rain was bliss. Someone had thrown a blanket over me, but it was getting drenched too. I started shivering.

A face loomed over me. 'Are you trying to die, or what?' But it was gone before I could work out an answer. Nearby, someone said, "Nil by mouth" and "pregnant", so I knew the talk was about me. I couldn't be bothered turning my head to see who spoke. After so long being held, supported and stationary, my muscles had atrophied and many of my joints had frozen. Any movement was a real pain—literally.

So, I lay in the rain and shivered, and tried to work out if I wanted to live or not.

How had things come to this?

Years ago, things were going fine. My wife and I ran a hotel on the northern outskirts of the business district. Not close enough to attract city rates, but close enough to attract business lunches in our little restaurant, and the odd office worker staying overnight. We weren't rolling in cash, and it was hard work, but we were making enough to pay our small staff and even save a little.

Then she got pregnant and tried to tell me it was mine. But I knew it wasn't.

Way back, when I was an impoverished student, I'd tried to sell my sperm to one of those sperm banks. They paid me, thanked me, and told me never to darken their doors again. Like all law students I was a bit of a litigious bastard back then and I pushed until they were forced to tell me why.

I shoot blanks.

By the time I recovered from that shock, I'd been kicked out of law school and spent the best part of two years just bumming around Australia. I came to my senses working behind the bar of what was to become my pub, when the current owner died some years later. I married the maitre d', and, like I said, things went along fine for quite a while.

I told her I didn't care. I didn't. I really didn't. This was the only way I was ever going to have children, after all. I thought of it like artificial insemination with a donor dad, except it wasn't artificial. Big deal. I was prepared to give the kid my name and help bring it up. What more could I do?

She couldn't handle it though. Not the guilt of sleeping around. I think she'd been offering our customers a little extra on the side since before I arrived. Not that. It was the knowing that I knew that she couldn't handle. I could see it every time she looked at me, until she couldn't look anymore, and one day I woke up to find her gone; and our savings with her.

It's even harder work running a pub on your own, and the downhill slide had already set in when the Aliens invaded.

There's a large park between us and the city proper. They landed there, took one look at my largely empty three-storey building, decided it was a perfect stop off point for their troops, and placed me and my four staff members under the control of one of their people.

"She" had a way of making one obey. With a gesture, she could direct one's blood anywhere in the body she pleased. She could starve the brain, or engorge certain organs, whatever took her fancy.

I obeyed. My staff obeyed. Until they ran away.

Drander punished me, of course. Oh, she was furious. I found out she couldn't just move blood around; she could also change its temperature. Oh, God, that hurt. But it wasn't my fault. How could it be? Drander slept in my bed. With me. I had become totally isolated from my staff. A really effective divide and conquer technique. My staff weren't going to confide in me. I knew nothing. Eventually she accepted this and stopped. She even had the grace to apologise. I repaid that by vomiting on her. That's when I learnt that her belt could be used as a whip and it could be mobilised in a second. I still carry the scar across my right cheek from the nose down to the base of the jawbone under the ear.

I yelled at her. That whipping was just so unfair.

She blinked in surprise.

'We have the [General] and his staff coming for tea. You better work out how to feed twenty people before they get here.'

Then she left me and my poor abused body to clean up and cope as best I could, while she sorted out the linen, and the table settings.

I should explain Drander and the [General] and the other Aliens. They seemed to come in multiple forms. Drander had skin like us Humans but greenish in colour. Her body was completely hairless and if she had genitalia, I had yet to work out what it was or where. I thought of her as female. I needed to think of her as female because of the things she had me doing. The face was a bit insect-like despite the skin. The mouth was small, and the lips came to a point which protruded outwards, like she was permanently making a moue. The ears and nose were mere holes in the skull, roughly where ours are. The eyes however were huge in that bare skull. Huge black pupils in a velvety purple iris. Hardly any white at all. They absorbed light so well that she needed triple eyelids to protect them. She was actually kind of cute to look at—if you could forget she was the enemy and had the power of life or death over you, that is. When she blinked, eyelids one and two would come up and down with such rapidity they would almost trip over each other in their haste. When she got angry her skin turned a bronze colour, the amount of anger indicated by how dark it was. And compared to the others, her kind were small; Human sized.

The [General], on the other hand, was always that dark bronze colour, and his skin was hard and cold, like a snake's. His ears were long and pointed and could swivel in any direction. His mouth was a huge teethy gash across his face, like a crocodile's, and he wasn't above baring those pointy monstrosities at any minion who got in his way. Even by the Aliens' standards he was tall, about nine feet high, where most of his kind stood just above eight feet. I thought of them as male because they were soldiers. Sexist of me perhaps, but it made it easier for me if I assigned a gender to them.

My pub had been built centuries ago in the days of gas lights, so the ceilings were high, about twelve feet, and this was one of the reasons they had picked it. They still had to stoop to come through the doors though.

The other kind hardly ever left the ship. They were as tall as the [General], but so skinny they were barely even skeletons. They didn't like exposing themselves to Earth's atmosphere. Drander just called them "[the ship people]" and ignored them. On occasion I had to go across the park to one of the ships to collect supplies, so I probably saw more of them than any other Human. They were so tall, so skinny, and their skin was so dry they reminded me more of praying mantises than people. When standing outside the ship, they always had their first eyelid down giving them a blind look, but I knew from experience with Drander that they could see perfectly well with the first eyelid down and never took any chances with them.

Today, having twenty plus Aliens for tea, was one of those times. So, I grabbed the trolley and dragged my aching body across the park. Usually the stuff I needed was already waiting for me, but I must have been early because one of [the ship people] was just depositing the containers. It paused and watched me coming closer. Ordinarily I would have waited until it had gone back inside but I was still angry with Drander and marched right up to it and glared, daring it to do something, anything, so I could break its skinny body in two.

Nobody likes a collaborator, and it seemed the Aliens in the ship were no exception because the next thing I knew a big globule of spit had landed on my cheek, right on the whip lash. It hurt like hell. I screamed and put my hand up. It chittered like a cricket, knocked my hand away, and smeared the spit along the cut. Then it kind of flew up the ramp into the ship. The ramp withdrew, with me still gaping after it.

I put my hand up again and felt my cheek. The spit had dried into a wax-like substance, which had adhered all along the lash, forming a malleable protective barrier. It had stopped hurting too. So had the rest of my body. Wondering, I loaded up the trolley and dragged it back to the hotel.

Drander waited at the kitchen entrance for me, but she stepped aside when she saw me dragging the trolley and let me in.

Did she think I was going to run away too? Where to?

This was my hotel, my home. Millions of refugees tramped the roads all over the country looking for someplace the Aliens hadn't reached. There just wasn't any such place. My staff should have realised that, but they couldn't bring themselves to work for the Aliens. It wasn't pleasant, it wasn't fun, but I still had a home and food in my belly. Locals no longer frequented my pub, and no-one paid me anymore, but I was still doing the same work I'd been doing for years.

We got a dozen refugees every day coming to the back door and begging us for food or other handouts as they drifted from one place to another. Now my staff were amongst their number. I understood. I bore them no animosity, but I did need to replace them.

In the kitchen, I unpacked the Alien food containers. Awful stuff. The main contents were a slimy lump, a dark purple in colour and smelling foul, like all their food. You treated it like meat, but cooked it for about half as long. There was also a small container within which was a block of yellow wobbly stuff. This was a great delicacy we served in very small quantities with a dribble of chocolate or a berry coulis to fill up the plate. Once, one of our customers had left theirs uneaten and we had all tried it. Drander showed no sympathy when we spent the next 24 hours vomiting. Said it served us right for stealing food. Personally, I think she was annoyed we got to it before her. Or maybe she was annoyed we hadn't shared it with her.

'What did you do?' She had come back into the kitchen and was watching me unpack.

'Huh?'

She touched her cheek. '[The ship people] don't waste that on just anyone.'

I touched my cheek too and fingered the wax-like covering. There was a mirror over the sink. Where I'd had a bright red cut which probably should have had stitches, I now had a dark green raised welt, rising smoothly from my skin.

I shook my head. 'I don't know. What is it?'

'It heals.'

My jaw dropped. 'I was ready to kill it. Why would it do that for me?'

'You were what?' She raised her hand in a familiar gesture. 'No-one'—and then again for emphasis—'no-one touches [the ship people].'

I bit my lip and shrank against the sink, not daring to look her in the eye. 'You need me,' I whispered desperately.

She made a sound with her lips which indicated displeasure. 'I need someone. There are twenty million of you out there. I can conscript someone else.'

Startled, I looked up. 'My Hotel.'

'Whose?'

Defiant, I repeated firmly, 'My Hotel.'

'My hotel, worm. And don't you forget it.'

She grabbed the cutlery tray and stalked out.

Maybe I should join the runaways. I grabbed the shopping list and headed for the door.

I didn't make it.

Behind me I heard her click her fingers. The blood started pumping from my heart out of sequence. It felt like a vice was gripping my chest as my heart tried to return to its proper rhythm. Somehow, I managed to hold up the shopping list. She plucked it out of my hand and let my own heart take over again. Gently. Too fast, and I would have fainted. She'd learnt that the first day.

'Nice try,' she commented, and contacted someone on her wrist phone.

I didn't understand a word, but it was obvious she was phoning the order in. I stood there trying to breathe without pain. Shallow breaths which wouldn't put any pressure on my chest. In. Out. Trying to match the beating of my straining heart.

She finished her call and looked closely at me. Hand on my shoulder, I could feel her taking over, but this time she was slowing my heart back to its proper rhythm, orchestrating the blood to flow in the proper sequence. Putting things back the way they should be. Absurdly, even knowing she was responsible, I felt gratitude.

She dropped her hand and stepped back. 'I'm sure you can find something useful to do.'

I could, of course. There was always something which needed doing. I followed her out of the kitchen, but where she went straight ahead to continue setting the tables, I turned right and went behind the bar and started checking the stock levels after the previous night. We got no locals coming in during lunch any longer, and no afternoon beer drinkers. The Aliens liked spirits, coffee, and red wine, especially of the fortified varieties, so those were all I checked. I had a feeling the beer was close to its use-by date, but with no-one drinking it, it seemed better to leave it where it was than throw it out.

The groceries arrived while I was down in the cellar, so I got on with the cooking when I finished in the bar. The [General]'s twenty had already chosen what they wanted to eat, so they were relatively easy to deal with. It was the dozen or so clients without a reservation who may or may not turn up who caused the most problems. And I had to change the á la carte menu. I was a competent enough cook, but I was no chef, and I knew I couldn't do everything on the current menu.

The computer was in the bar, so I went back there when I finished preparing that purple stuff and the vegetables. The ovens and the fryer were on, and I was just waiting for them to get hot enough. Drander came over to see what I was up to. She frowned as I wiped out line after line. I stopped what I was doing and waited for her to say something.

'Add <some Alien word>.'

I frowned at her. 'I have no idea what that is. I don't even know if I can spell it.'

'Our clients know. It's not hard.' She reached out and took over the keyboard.

I moved aside and let her. In the finish, between what she could cook and what I could cook, we still had a respectable menu, even if I didn't recognise half the meals. I printed it out and she started changing over the menus on the tables. I went back to the kitchen.

I was interrupted several times by our regular stream of refugees. If Drander was in the room I sent them packing, otherwise I slipped them some of the previous day's untouched food. Food Regulations said I wasn't allowed to use it, but there was nothing wrong with it. Better it went to our people than into a bin.

At one point I attempted to take the garbage out. As I stepped through the door, it felt like I'd slammed into a brick wall. Rubbing my sore nose, I turned back inwards.

'Uh, Drander, Ma'am?'

'I thought I made it clear. You are confined to the hotel.'

Mutely I held up the garbage bag. She made that annoyed sound and frowned at me. Then she spoke to someone on her wrist phone, came over, and taking the bag off me, took it out to the bins.

As she came back in, I muttered, 'You're doing all the washing, are you?' then clutched my ears as the blood roared into them.

But she was just chiding me for my rudeness. It was gone in a second. We both got back to work.

There were only four others who arrived without a booking, all of them Drander's kind. I think the [General]'s party frightened them because they sat right next to the door, had a main course, and left. And Drander was right, the unpronounceable thing was popular and easy to prepare. It was basically deep-fried purple stuff in a potato batter, cooked until the batter was a crispy golden colour and the purple stuff inside was merely warm. All four chose it and ate with relish before scarpering.

Our party of twenty were a lot more demanding and kept us both scuttling between the kitchen and the bar and the table for hours. The first time I brought anything to their table, the [General] grabbed my face and looked long and hard at my cheek. By the time he released me, my neck hurt from being tilted back so far for so long. If he made any comment though, he made it to Drander, not me.

We were clearing up when someone else came through the front door. It was one of Drander's kind again, and he was carrying something concealed under his overcoat. Drander appeared to know him and they sat down together talking. From under his coat, he pulled what looked like the sort of guns they use to tranquilise zoo animals, a short wide barrel with a small handle.

Drander called, 'Come here,' to me.

I looked at the gun, and I looked at them, and I shook my head. Drander blinked. The other Alien stood up, leaving the gun on the table, and came closer to me. All my instincts said "run", but I held still and let him. He too seemed extraordinarily interested in my cheek. Then he turned back to Drander and was obviously remonstrating with her. As the argument got more heated, I took the opportunity and fled back to the kitchen, where I started doing the dishes. With no kitchen hand, these had been piling up all night, and there were mountains of them to do before we could retire. Luckily, it hadn't been a full house.

They caught up with me as I was pulling the first tray of clean glasses off the conveyer belt. With my back to the machine and my arms full, I could only watch as they approached.

He held the gun thing up. I put the tray between us.

'Drander, please?' I said.

'It's just a tag,' she said, disgusted.

A tag? So, she would always know where I was? I shook my head at him and appealed to her. 'Don't, please.'

'You want to be free to leave the hotel, don't you?'

Not this way. 'If I promise not to run away?'

'What are you hiding?'

'Nothing.'

'Then what's the problem?'

'A tag. A tag is forever. This'—I waved the tray around to indicate the here and now—'this may not be.'

Two eyelids drooped, and she looked at me with narrowed eyes. Her skin grew darker. I'd not seen that look before. I didn't think I liked it.

'Please, Drander.' And, because I was beginning to understand that there was no real love lost between Drander's kind and the [General]'s kind, I said, 'There may come a time when you actually find me more useful untagged.'

'We are all tagged,' she responded but the skin colour was retreating. The third eyelid joined the inner two at the halfway mark.

The Alien with the gun tapped his cheek, pointed at me, and said something. She nodded, and he dropped his arm, so the gun was pointing downwards.

'Promise?'

I nodded. 'I promise not to run away from my hotel.'

The three eyelids flipped back up and she rolled her eyes. 'My hotel.' But she drew the gunman away and left me to the dishes.

She finished clearing the tables and took the linen out to the laundry, where she ironed and folded the previous day's linen while tonight's went through the washer. I had finished the dishes and was changing the oil in the deep fryer when she came back in.

She pulled a face at me. 'Wash before you come to bed,' she said, continuing through the kitchen.

It had never entered my head not to.

We shared a bed. My bed. When she first arrived, she claimed the room above the bar with its en-suite and a view of the street—my room—and unpacked her belongings. I attempted to pack mine and move elsewhere. She wouldn't let me. I attempted to sleep elsewhere. She fetched me back. I attempted to sneak out in the middle of the night. Pain convinced me to return. At first, I had lain beside her wide awake, unable to sleep, but exhaustion catches up with you. Now, it felt normal to crawl in beside her after my shower and prepare for sleep.

'Tomorrow, do something about replacing our staff,' she murmured as I lay down.

'You mean, later today,' I corrected her, it being well after midnight.

She thumped me, but gently. She was as exhausted as I was.

'Drander?'

'Hmm?'

'Why is everyone so interested in my cheek?'

'I told you. [The ship people] don't waste that on just anyone.'

'Why did it bother the guy with the tagging gun?'

She didn't answer.

'Drander?'

'Go to sleep.'

I sighed and rolled over. I don't know why she insisted on my company in bed. We didn't do anything except sleep. Of course, everyone thought otherwise, but I think she did it because she just simply hated being alone at night.

Like I said, no-one likes a collaborator, and as I walked down the street, people looked darkly at me, and, on occasion, someone would spit on the pavement as I passed, but they didn't dare touch me. They got to me in other ways like calling me "Alien lover" or "Ale" to my face, and doubling the price when they saw me coming. A month ago, these had been my friends and neighbours. I kept my mouth shut, my eyes lowered, and paid what I was asked to pay.

Profiteering might be a crime, but I wasn't about to report them to anyone, and Drander seemed able to afford it. We had no bookings for tonight, but we were expecting a full shipload of over one hundred staying overnight on the morrow, so I would come out again to the markets early the next day and get fresh produce for our guests. Other stuff, such as rice and coffee and alcohol, were still being delivered in bulk. Today's shop was mainly for things for me to eat like porridge and fresh bread, and real meat. Drander might nibble on left over purple stuff all day, but I couldn't bring myself to touch it.

As I headed back, I noticed the local Catholic school had re-opened. A small sign on the gate declared they would teach any child, prep to Year 10. Then in smaller print: "VCE and VCAL taught but not examined". These were the last two years which were used as preparation for further education such as University. Then in larger letters: "Daily fee covers 2 meals and a snack". Then a really modest fee was mentioned. Even multiplied out by two hundred (the number of school days in a normal year) it was a fraction of what this once exclusive school had been charging before the Aliens arrived. So many businesses had closed, and so many people were drifting about as refugees, I still wondered how many kids could actually afford those rates—even with meals thrown in. Still I was glad to see some kids would have a future when/if the Aliens left.

My first refugee of the day was a known fugitive. His picture was up on our notice board.

Drander was in the laundry so I dragged him in and showed it to him. He had been a sous-chef at the Ritz in another city. He was responsible for poisoning some of the [General]'s kind.

He went white. 'I didn't mean to. I didn't know.'

'What did you give them?'

He shrugged. 'Prawns.'

'What?'

'Garlic prawns. They were fresh! There was nothing wrong with them. *We* ate them without a problem,' he said.

'I've never given our customers crustacean before,' I mused aloud. We had that purple stuff.

'Your ... your customers?'

'Yeah.' I looked him in the eye and waved my hand around. 'You've come begging at the wrong door. This hotel is under Alien management.'

He went even whiter. 'They said you'd feed me. Everyone said you were generous with food.'

Oh, did they? 'Who's they?'

'The others on the road. They said you were good for a meal.'

'Are we? No-one warned you?'

He shook his head.

'We have a basement ...' I began.

What the hell was I doing? Just because Drander had never been down there didn't mean she wouldn't. How long could I feed him without her knowing? She had a disturbing habit of knowing exactly what I was thinking. This was so dangerous, but the Genie was out of the bottle now.

He stunk so bad I almost gagged as he swept me up in a bear hug. Hastily I pushed him off and took him through the kitchen and down to our basement. It used to be a coal cellar, but now I used it for bulk sacks of potatoes and rice and wheat flour and stuff like that. They could be delivered directly from the truck and down the old coal chute without having to be carried into the hotel. Because it had been a coal cellar, the people working here used to get dirty and someone had installed a sink and running water a century or so ago, so it was ideal for someone hiding out, if they could only stay out of sight.

I went back upstairs, filched some blankets from the pile Drander was making in the hallway, and went back down with some of my bread and cheese, and a jug of milk. He had already started rearranging the sacks, so they created a hidey hole out of sight of both the stairs and the coal hole. I left him to it, hoping I hadn't done him or myself a massive disservice.

At least now I knew why we got so many refugees coming to our door. Word had gotten around. My staff had obviously been as guilty as me in the manner we disposed of our leftovers.

Well, messages could be spread both ways.

To the next refugee who arrived, I mentioned our need for staff. When they protested about working for the enemy, I pointed out that the more Human staff the place had, the more likely they, the refugees, were of getting a feed out of us. I went on to point out there'd be lots of leftovers the day after tomorrow—but not if we had to take in Alien help.

Half an hour later, a boy in his late teens knocked on our door. He stood there awkwardly looking down at his worn-out shoes, his long unkempt fair hair hiding a thin pimply face. No way would I have considered him a month ago, but now I waited for him to speak.

'I've come ... I mean ... I heard ...' He looked up at me, and said in a rush, 'Please can my Mum and I have the job?'

'Your Mum?' I scanned the yard. There, hiding near the bins, two heads. 'And who else?'

He yelped, turned around and frantically waved them back into hiding.

Behind me, Drander blew a series of small raspberries. With her kind this signified amusement. In mine, of course, it meant something totally different. He mistook it and swung back around flinching but prepared to defend them. I liked his spirit.

'Tell them to come in,' Drander said and led the way inside.

The woman was large, but the way the clothes hung off her, she'd been at least two sizes larger once. Trailing her, and hiding behind her skirts was a young girl, maybe eight or nine.

Drander frowned at the child. 'You are too young to work.'

'She can help,' said the mother anxiously. 'She won't eat much.'

Drander shook her head, still frowning. 'You should be in school, shouldn't you?'

I licked my lips. Just how deep were Drander's pockets? 'There's a school about a block away. It's not free, but it is open for business. They'll even feed her there.'

'And you know this, because?'

'I went past there this morning. It's between here and the supermarket.' As Drander raised an eyebrow, I remembered too late that I hadn't actually asked permission before wandering off. 'I was hungry. I wanted stuff I could eat,' I growled out through gritted teeth.

'Did you buy enough to share with them?'

Between me and the sous-chef there wasn't much of the bread left, but I nodded anyway.

'You will work,' she said to the child, 'but you will also go to school. School comes first.'

'Oh, thank you, thank you, Sir,' gasped out the mother, bowing to Drander and attempting to grasp her hand.

'What can you do?' Drander asked her, stepping out of the way of her enthusiasm.

'Me?'

Drander nodded.

'Oh, um. Cook, clean, make beds, sew.'

'General factotum, in other words. A domestic,' I said.

Only Drander acknowledged that I'd spoken, the others having eyes only for her.

A hotel is yours in name only, if the staff are not yours. If we employed these people, they would be hers, not mine. And that would make it her hotel. Defeated, I prepared to walk away. I had promised not to run away from my hotel. I hadn't said anything about hers.

I couldn't do it though. I felt so heart-sick at that point, I wanted to, but I couldn't abandon the sous-chef. I would just have to live with it.

'Worm?'

Why did she always call me that? I found it so demeaning. She hadn't called any of my previous staff "worm". Just me. I stopped, but I refused to show her my face. She came around and stood directly in front of me, mere inches from my nose. I refused to meet her eyes.

'What are you doing?' she asked softly.

'Your hotel,' I replied.

'Your people.'

I shook my head. 'Your staff.'

She looked unconvinced.

'Look at them,' I said.

She did, and comprehension dawned. 'Interview the boy,' she said.

'And split the family?'

'There won't be a split if we act of one accord.'

'You mean, if I do what you tell me to?'

The two eyelids dropped again, and that narrow-eyed stare confronted me again. 'Bar and Kitchen—your domain. The rest—mine.'

I gasped. What a really generous offer from someone who believed the whole kit and caboodle belonged to them. It was also, give or take, the split my wife and I had had. There was still a huge area of overlap, but experience said it could work—if we acted of one accord.

'Our hotel,' she said and reached up, smoothing the waxy covering on my cheek.

I could feel my blood rising to meet her fingertips. She didn't seem to be aware of the impact she was having, so I gently removed her fingers before it became painful.

'Our hotel,' I agreed.

If the kitchen were mine, then the sous-chef had a better chance. I just had the kid to worry about.

We turned back to the waiting family. 'Have you warned her what her first twenty-four hours will entail?' I asked. 'Is she up for it?'

Drander considered, then nodded, and went on to explain to the mother how we would have over a hundred guests descending on us, and every room in the hotel had to cleaned and stocked, and every bed made up with fresh linen before noon the next day.

She blanched, took a deep breath. 'I'll work around the clock if I have to,' she announced staunchly.

'Good, 'cause we just may be,' Drander told her.

My turn. 'And what can you do for us?' I asked the boy.

Confused, he looked from one of us to the other and then to his mother. She nodded encouragement and he turned back, this time to me. Not stupid, this one. 'I'm a second-year apprentice.'

'Papers?'

He looked at the ground and shook his head.

'Area?'

'Oh, um, pastry chef.'

'Not much call for that in a pub restaurant,' I said.

His eyes fell again.

'What I need is a fully qualified chef—which you are not—and a kitchen hand to peel spuds and scrub pots and pans. And tomorrow we will be feeding a hundred and six people lunch and tea, and breakfast the next day. Oh, and they're not Human people.'

'They'll be mostly <something>,' Drander added. I knew the word to mean the [General]'s people, even if I couldn't pronounce it.

'Big, eight-foot-tall crocodile people,' I said.

Drander blew a raspberry and covered her mouth, blinking rapidly.

He knew who we meant, because he paled. 'I can scrub pans, Sir,' he said.

Drander and I looked at each other.

'First they scrub themselves,' I said.

She agreed.

'Do we have three spare beds for them?'

'I can offer you a double room with a trundle bed for the next two nights, then we can sort you out with something more permanent. I am Drander. This is 'Ale'. And he calls me 'Ma'am', not 'Sir'.'

When had she heard that nickname? Did she know what it was short for? Still, it was better than 'Worm', so I held my peace. They turned out to be Sean, Enya (the mother), and Rita. Introductions over, they headed off with Drander to get clean.

Sean scrubbed up okay, but he didn't have a change of clothes, so I grabbed him and his sister, and we headed off to the nearest cheap clothes outlet still operating. From the look on their faces, this was a form of slumming they hadn't anticipated. Tough. I wasn't wasting time or money hunting up the sort of boutique clothing they seemed to feel they should be getting. I just wanted "clean" in my kitchen. And for good measure, in my coal cellar as well. If/when their mum got time, she could sew them something more to their liking.

Enya and the sous-chef were appropriately grateful, even if the kids weren't.

Back in the kitchen, Sean and I got to work doing what preparation we could for the coming twenty-four hours. Desserts could be pre-prepared and stored in the fridges. He had a nice deft hand when it came to swirling blended yellow stuff through milk rice. And he took me seriously when I told him to keep his hands very clean and not try to eat the stuff.

He gagged when I pulled the purple stuff out of the fridge and put it on the bench ready for slicing and marinating. I empathised entirely, but it was a luxury we didn't have time for.

'How thin can you slice?'

He shook his head. 'I've never handled a meat knife,' he said, 'I'm only second year.'

So, I set him to chopping tomatoes and onions and garlic for the sauce, and started slicing into the awful stuff myself.

'What is it?' The sous-chef, in his clean clothes, had crept up the stairs and was watching from the shadows.

I checked behind me to make sure Drander hadn't crept in too.

'Relax. I can see both doors from here and get out of the way in a hurry, if I have to.'

Reassured, I answered him quietly, so as not to draw Sean's attention to us.

'I call it "that god-awful purple stuff". Drander calls it,' and I tried, somewhat unsuccessfully, to repeat the sounds she produced when referring to it.

That was my first attempt to say anything in her language. Oddly, after that my ears suddenly became attuned to the different sounds involved. Not long after that I started picking out individual words.

'What do you do with it?'

I explained as I continued cutting. With over a hundred soldiers all eating at the same time, we had decided on a limited range of options. I was currently creating thin slices that would be marinated for at least an hour and then stir fried and used in a salad for their lunch when they arrived. Their options were limited to a choice of three marinades, and what they drank with it. Until each option ran out, that is.

'I can do that a lot faster and thinner than you.'

'Probably.' I grunted. 'After all, you're a Chef, I'm just a cook. I'm not even that, really. I'm a barman.' And then I looked up at him. 'And how do you propose to do it without someone seeing you?'

He grimaced and agreed. I got back to work, trusting him to keep himself hidden. I had a restaurant to run. But he did help, sneaking out when Sean's back was turned and stirring sauces or doing other small things, during the tea-time rush while Sean or Drander were out of the room and while I flitted between the kitchen and the bar. With only half a dozen couples, it was a relatively quiet night, which is what we needed before the chaos looming up.

The next morning, the wax stuff dissolved in the shower, leaving a smooth pink scar behind. In time it would fade to white, but unlike most scars there was no sign of puckering, and it has remained as malleable as any normal flesh. Drander looked ghastly this morning. The inner eyelid seemed to be glued three quarters shut and her normal greenish tint was more grey than green. But then she'd had only half the amount of sleep that I'd had.

'Ready?' I asked her, and she nodded.

'You?'

'No. There's a lot I couldn't do till today.'

She nodded, gave me a brief hug. 'You'll manage,' she said and headed into the bathroom, leaving me touching my shoulder in shock.

What the hell? Where had that come from? She had changed. I didn't know if it was because I'd finally yelled back and been standing up for myself, or because [the ship person] had marked me, or because she'd had to take on the role of worker as well as controller in the last few days. Whatever the reason, she was different now. I gave myself a mental shake. I didn't have time for this.

'What happened?' Sean asked, as I dragged him out of bed and down to the Fruit and Veg market.

'Whaddyamean?'

'Your cheek.'

'Whip lash.'

'What?'

'They carry whips.'

'Who?'

'The Aliens.'

'Oh.' He digested that as he followed me around doing his undernourished seventeen-year-old best to be a pack horse.

'Sir?'

'Yeah?'

'Is my sister safe?'

Safe? Safe was a relative term these days. 'Keep her out of the way of the customers. Especially the [General]'s kind. They're soldiers.'

He looked blank.

'The big crocodile people.'

'Oh. And Miss Drander's kind?'

'I don't know. But they are not as harmless as they look.' I looked him in the eye and said earnestly, 'If you get on the wrong side of any of the Aliens, they will hurt you. All of them.'

He nodded seriously. 'K ... Kill?'

'They have that ability. I haven't seen it, but I know they can.'

Someone spat at us as they went past.

Sean jumped. 'Who was that?'

I looked at the retreating back and sighed. 'Our next-door neighbour.'

'What?'

'The luggage repairs place. Used to be a regular customer till the Aliens took over.' I felt the bile rise in my own throat and spat too. 'Come on. We have work to do.'

After the market I headed to the Supply Ship. I left Sean behind peeling and boiling potatoes to make the potato batter and did that trip on my own. The Troop carrier was already there, but still sealed up. We had three hours before they came across to us. [The ship person] was waiting for me. It beckoned and I readily went up to it this time. It ran a finger along the scar and chittered to itself.

'Thank you,' I said.

It tilted its head and I found myself looking at a long thin eye in the side of its head. It looked opaque because the inner eyelid was down. I repeated myself. I didn't know if it understood, and I resolved to ask Drander how to say it properly. This time I saw the wings unfurl from that impossibly skinny frame and watched as it flew up.

'What did it say?'

I was on the floor pulling out a fungus-like vegetable, which would be a major ingredient in the

salad. It liked cool dark places, so we stored it on the
floor in the cool room. 'I don't speak chitter,' and I
tried to emulate the sound it had made for her.

Drander laughed, which meant blowing raspberries
at me, startling Sean, but he was getting used to it.

'You just said,' she informed me, '"don't be stupid
next time". Or a very good approximation of that.'

I sat back on my haunches, gaping up at her. 'Come
again?'

She repeated the chittering sound I'd been trying to
emulate. 'That it?'

'Yeah. I ... I think so. You mean it was actually
talking *to* me?'

'What? You think it was talking to the empty air?'

'Um.' I had actually. I flushed as I realised how
arrogant that had been.

She rolled her eyes and started to leave.

'Uh, Drander? Ma'am?'

She half turned back. Her eyelids had retreated to
their proper place, but she still looked tired.

'How do you say "Thank you" in your language?' I
asked her.

She stared at me. Those two eyelids came halfway
down again. I began to realise this meant she was
thinking deeply. What had I said? She shook her head.
'You ... don't.'

'What?'

She frowned. 'There's just no way to express that.'
She sounded troubled. As well, she might. What sort of
society never thanked anybody?

Still looking troubled, she headed back out to the restaurant with a tray of cutlery. Come to think of it, I had never heard her thank me either. She had lots of ways of expressing her displeasure, most of them painful, but on the rare occasions I had pleased her, all I'd got was a quick pat on the shoulder. Maybe, if I hadn't flinched every time she'd done it, there might have been more, but in the light of what she'd just said, I doubted it. Ironic, I thought. The first thing I tried to say in their language was something that couldn't be said.

Then the Alien hordes descended, and Drander sent Rita into the kitchen, out of harm's way, and I had to attend to the bar. Our guests appreciated the lunch being a blend of the familiar and the exotic, they appreciated a sky over their heads and being on terra firma again, but mostly they appreciated the (for them) free sampling of the delights of Earthly alcohol.

We had to close the bar for an hour, so I could get back into the kitchen to cook tea. Their CO sent them out, ordering them to get some sun on their skins before it went down. I prayed the locals had the sense to stay out of their way.

Then the madness started again. We were doing the deep-fried purple stuff on a bed of wilted (officially blanched) silverbeet for entrée. Drander said the flavours complemented each other. Main course was roasted purple stuff, and some root vegetable which came from the ships and looked like an orange turnip but tasted like a bitter sweet potato and some Earth based vegetables. I'd also chucked a small roast lamb in for us Humans when/if we had time to eat.

We were "Busy"' with a capital "B", when Drander came in and ordered me to reopen the bar. I knew she was right, but I just didn't see how I was going to manage it. When the Chef slipped out from the stairwell and said, 'Go.' I was so grateful all I did was snap "Whites" at him as I stripped off my apron and headed for the bar.

Drander grabbed me and slammed me against the wall in the small passage between the public area and the kitchen. 'What are you doing? You know who that is?'

The blood started singing in response, just enough pulled away from the brain to make me dizzy. I pulled her hand away from my heart. 'My kitchen, my domain.' I snarled at her. 'You want me in the bar, or not?'

She slapped me. 'What if they see him?' she said, jerking her head back to the restaurant.

'You know nothing.' I snarled. 'The kitchen is my domain, remember? You've never seen him. You've never spoken to him. Understood?'

That double eyelid look again, and my blood stopped misbehaving.

'How long have you been hiding him?'

'You know nothing,' I repeated.

She actually smiled and patted my shoulder. 'It is time you earnt your untagged status, worm.'

What the hell? What had I unleashed? Suddenly she terrified me as she hadn't managed to do before. I leant against the wall trembling as I watched her go back into the kitchen. She spoke to Sean, carefully averting her face away from the Chef, and collected a tray of entrees. I fled for the bar before she found me loitering still.

A couple of hours or so into the meal, when the crowd had received their main meal and were busy chomping away, Sean brought me out a plate of roast lamb and Earth based vegetables.

'Your mum?' I asked.

'Miss Drander took a plate to her.'

I pulled a jug of soft drink and handed it to him. 'For the kitchen.'

He grinned and thanked me. I managed to get most of my meal eaten before the post-meal orders started rolling in.

Then the CO got up and talked to them. I assumed it was about what to expect and how to behave, etc, etc. It seemed the logical thing for him to be saying to them. By concentrating really hard I was able to discern where one word ended, and another started but I didn't understand any of it. Then the desserts came out and the night rolled on.

I closed the bar at midnight and went to help with the clean up. It was mostly done, even the frying fat change over. As the most junior member of staff, Sean was dealing with it, reluctantly and with much muttering and dark looks in our direction, but he was doing it.

'Want a beer when you finish?' I asked.

He perked up enormously, just as I realised he was still underage. What the hell, the offer was made, and someone had to drink it. He'd definitely earnt it.

'What's your poison?' I asked the Chef.

'How good's your port?'

'Usual pub stuff. Got some 'Federation' laid down for a special occasion, but this isn't it.'

He laughed. It was good to hear real Human laughter in the kitchen again. I got their drinks and one for me, and we started work on breakfast.

Drander and Enya came through with the dirty tablecloths. Drander took my drink away from me with a frown. From the daggers Enya was sending towards her son, I think she wanted to do the same.

'Missus got you over the barrel?' asked Chef.

'She is not my Missus.'

Sean and he openly grinned at each other. I rolled my eyes and wished for the floor to swallow me up.

'Where's Rita?' I asked to change the subject.

'We sent her to bed after the desserts were served,' Chef said. 'She could hardly put one foot in front of the other. It was getting dangerous to have her about.'

Made sense. They got her to help with the stuff which had a finite time constraint, then let her go when they got up to the less urgent stuff. We all needed sleep, but she, being a kid, needed it more than the rest of us, and we'd obviously exhausted her.

Soon we would all be able to go to bed, except that meant confronting Drander and her mysterious threat. I swayed and leant against the bench. Chef, looking concerned, offered me his glass, but I waved him away. If Drander didn't want me drinking, then drinking was probably not a good idea. I bottled the emotion and told him what needed to be done with the sweet potato flavoured turnip to turn it into a breakfast dish—sort of a cross between pancakes and a Spanish omelette—served cold with condiments. They were fond of soy sauce, and a really smelly creation made with the fungus stuff and garlic.

When the ladies came back through with clean linen, we were all hard at work in different parts of the kitchen—Sean was peeling vegetables, Chef was mixing batter, and I—once again relegated to the Alien foodstuffs—was dicing fungus stuff. Drander nodded her approval, which earnt her a glare, as she popped a peeled garlic clove in her mouth.

'You make sure you clean your teeth before you come to bed!' I said.

She just blew a raspberry, mouthed [later] at me, and moved on.

'Ale, sir?' Chef was staring after them.

'Yeah?'

'That was ... garlic.'

'Yes. They're very fond of garlic.'

'Um ...'

I realised what he was trying to say without alerting Sean. 'I think it was the prawns. We've never given them prawns here. Fish, yes, but not crustaceans. It's been really hard to get hold of stuff like that.'

'What has?' Sean wanted in on the conversation.

'Prawns.'

'Good. I'm allergic to the stuff.'

'And you want to run a patisserie when this is over?' Chef commented.

If it ever is over, I thought, and tuned the two of them out. I was pretty certain it was "later" that Drander had mouthed at me in her language, but even if it wasn't, I wanted whatever it was to stop messing my night up.

I beat her to bed and was so tired I actually fell asleep waiting for her.

'Up.'

I checked my phone. 'It's 03:30.' I'd had just over two hours sleep. I groaned.

'Up. Now.'

Someone spoke in the darkness in our room, and it wasn't Drander! I was sitting upright before I recognised the voice—the gunman from the other night.

'It's you,' I said. 'How'd you get in?'

'I let him in. We have to talk.'

'Now?'

'[Yes, now],' he said, sitting on the end of the bed, and spoke some more to Drander, which I couldn't work out.

'[Yes]. He'll do it.'

Do what? I went to the toilet and came back and sat on the edge of the bed. They were still arguing. Did they always argue like this? 'Are you siblings?' I asked, recognising the nature of the bickering.

Drander laughed—her style. 'Closer. Batch siblings; from the same batch.'

'You are born in ... "batches"?'

'[Yes],' from him.

'We need your help with a batch.'

'Um?'

'Dr'gor,' Drander said, 'informs me they have started laying down batches here. We don't want this. Every planet we go, it happens. They invade. They drag us with them. They put us in charge. They raise batches of our children. Then they move on, taking our children with them. If we don't hold the place for them, our children suffer. If our parents don't hold the previous place, we suffer.'

Dr'gor said something.

'Those we invade hate us, the [General's people] hate us, [the ship people] despise us. But the [General's people] control our children, our parents, our home planet.'

If I'd been her, my two eyelids would have dropped halfway, as I thought about what she'd said. They were stuck between a rock and a hard place. If they rebelled, their families in the [General's people]'s control suffered up and down the line. But they couldn't rebel, because the locals wherever they stopped didn't differentiate between the different species of Aliens. To the locals, all Alien groups were equally anathema, and they would rather kill Drander's people on sight, than help them.

'What do you want me to do?' I asked at last.

'Destroy the batch.'

'But that's your children!'

Dr'gor spoke, 'Stop here, stop now. No more.'

'You want to be the last generation under their control?'

'[Yes].'

I turned the bedside light on and stared at them in consternation. They meant it, both of them.

'Is your baby amongst them?' I asked Drander.

She sucked her lips in. 'I can't. I am designated a ... a ... <something>. I cannot have my own children.'

Well, I knew all about that, and I found myself reaching for her hand.

Dr'gor spoke.

Drander translated. 'His baby is. That's why he knows. He knows where too.'

'And you want me to kill your baby?'

'Yessss.' Dr'gor pushed the unfamiliar word out with some difficulty.

'If I rescue them instead?'

'Too many. Cannot get near, help you. Tagged. They will know,' Dr'gor spoke slowly, carefully, not having his batchling's fluency with English.

'And if I rescue some?'

'If we are caught with them, lots of our people will die. Better the baby dies before sentience starts,' Drander explained.

I had no idea what that meant, but I figured I'd find out.

'You really want this?'

They both nodded, Dr'gor only a second behind Drander.

'Tonight?'

'Not far.'

'And how?'

'Burn?' Dr'gor asked.

I had a small torch downstairs for lighting brandy. It was fairly standard kitchen equipment, even if it didn't get used much here. I nodded.

I started getting dressed. I felt ill, and not just from exhaustion.

'You're asking me to murder—how many—children?'

Dr'gor spoke.

'He says two hundred. Maybe more. Batches come in tens.'

'You're asking me to kill at least two hundred babies?'

'Tagged.' There was something wrong with Dr'gor's eyes. A luminous rim at the base, which spilled over and ran down his face. Tears? 'No more. Stop now.'

'They'll know you came here,' I said.

He nodded. 'My job. Wander. Listen.'

'Spy.'

Drander agreed. 'His master is the [General]'s security chief. You've met him.'

'Master.' The word felt dirty in my mouth. 'Who is your master, Drander?'

'The [General].'

'I suppose I should feel honoured that I am owned by such a high-ranking slave,' I said. Neither reacted to the deliberate insult. 'What choice do I have?'

Dr'gor made a sound of annoyance, for which Drander gave him a look I'd not seen before.

'I won't force you. Not for this,' said Drander.

'So, I don't even get the Nuremburg Defence?'

'The what?'

'The "I was just doing what I was told" defence. Their deaths are going to be with me and weigh on my conscience forever.'

Dr'gor said something.

'Dr'gor just pointed out that we are at war, and this is an act of war,' Drander translated.

'They're babies. They can't be at war with us.'

'Um. More like worms at this stage. They have no sentience, no feelings, no senses. Dr'gor says they are not yet at the limb stage.'

'Meaning?'

She shrugged. 'What I said. They have no senses. They feel nothing. Um. If they were Human or [the General's people] they would still be carried inside.'

'Two hundred abortions then?'

She didn't know that word, but she did know a Human word which wasn't in her own language. 'Please, worm.'

With sudden clarity, I realised 'worm' was a term of endearment. She was saying, "Please, Babe", when she used it that way. It wasn't meant to be demeaning. Quite the opposite, in fact.

It annoyed Dr'gor to hear her use it on me though. He raised his voice at her and we both shushed him.

'There are a hundred and six of [the General's people] just above your head,' I snarled at him, 'You want to wake them up?'

He blinked rapidly at me. I don't know which surprised him more, the fact that I answered back or the fact that I could say that word. I knew I'd got it right, so I knew he knew what I'd said.

I sighed and sat back down. 'How long do I get to think about it?'

Another heated conversation. I recognised Drander saying [No] several times. Eventually Drander translated the gist of the conversation to me. 'They will develop limbs in a week. After that, it is murder. My people will still want it done.'

She paused to let that sink in. I just stared at the floor.

'He doesn't want to have to come back here on another night to show you where though.'

'Give me the address. I'll find it myself.'

Another conversation.

'He doesn't know the address. He knows the place. He stumbled on it doing his nightly wanders.'

I would've given the world to have just one child. To take it in my arms, hold its hand as it took its first stumbling steps. Anything, for just one child of my own. And here they were, asking me to kill two hundred of them.

'Drander,' I whispered, 'I ...'

She put her arms around me, and the blood sang in my veins, but not in a painful way.

'We'll find someone else. Go back to bed.'

Her brother hissed something with a query intonation at the end, probably asking "Who?" Yet another conversation. More [No]'s from Drander. It degenerated into a Yes/No quarrel between them.

I drifted off, but only for a few seconds. A power nap. When I woke up, my mind was clear. This was war, and every war had its share of casualties. It was going to happen anyway.

'Show me the place. What defences does it have?'

And then I realised I had nothing suitable to wear. I spent most of my time in kitchen whites.

Sensing this, Drander rummaged in her drawers and came up with a charcoal hoodie in a thick silky substance. Softer than wool and much lighter than it looked, it was a bit warm for so early in a Melbourne autumn, but would have to do.

Dr'gor took me across the road to the park and past the dark ships. In the park, on the city side, there was a bunker which the government had built in some forgotten war for city people to hide in, on the off chance that our town was ever under attack. Well, our town was overrun, and it seemed the enemy used the bunker as a nursery. Very ironic, that.

He left me there and continued on into the city.

It was a bunker built to withstand external attack. I had to actually get inside to torch anything. It had been some months since the invasion and whoever used to maintain the park seemed to have ceased to do so. I was able to wriggle up almost to the doors in the long grass. It wasn't guarded, but it was locked. It was an old lock though, the sort that responded to credit cards being slipped in from the right angle. The lock clicked open damaging my card, but it wasn't as though I could use it for anything else. No-one accepted credit any longer, not even us.

Once inside, I was confronted with a long corridor with doors on both sides. There was no-one around, so I methodically checked each door in turn. The first two rooms were just glorified closets.

In the third I found the babies.

Long rows of nests on benches. Each nest held a cream coloured, segmented creature, about as long as my forearm and twice as wide. A brown strip ran across one end of each creature. Just below the strip, a tube came out of a small slit. The tubes ran around the room and were attached to a large vat at the far end of the room. I couldn't bring myself to torch the babies directly, so I melted what must be feeding tubes as they gathered closer together near the vat. And moved on to the next room. And the next. In each room about two hundred nests, five rooms all up. In the last room buds were just forming where legs would be. I started crying, but by now I was operating on automatic. I torched the tubes, and then the vat for good measure. And then I torched the wooden doors on my way out, praying the babies inside were already dead. I could smell the tiny fires igniting flesh within each room.

I lay in the grass crying for some time before I felt the dry feathery touch of the skeletal creatures from the ship. They lifted me up and flew me back to my end of the park in silence. Four of them. When they landed, one of them prised open my mouth and spat inside. I swallowed before I realised what I was doing. And then they were gone.

Feeling physically better, I strode across the road to the hotel and was let in by an anxious Drander.

'One Thousand. There were one thousand babies in there,' I said to her. And suddenly I just had to get clean. I felt I had the blood of those thousand babies on my hands, covering my skin, in my hair, and on my clothes. I just had to get rid of it. I started stripping off as she hustled me back into our room. She locked our door and tried to help me, but I couldn't bear anyone touching me. I had murdered one thousand little babies. It didn't matter that they were Aliens. They were just tiny helpless babies and I ... I had killed them.

I slapped her hand away and rushed into the bathroom. I ended up in the shower half-dressed still and just let the water run over me, long after it ceased to be warm. Eventually the trembling ceased, and I began to feel numb, emotionally and physically. It was a long time after that before I moved.

Drander was asleep on the floor by the bathroom door, so I picked her up and put her to bed. The clock said 5:30, meaning I had to be up in half an hour anyway, so I got dressed and took our clothes out to the laundry. Mine stank. I came to associate that rank smell with death and fear. I should have been dropping with exhaustion, but I had been feeling physically fine since I swallowed [the ship person]'s spit. I wondered how long it would last and was once again grateful to them. If I couldn't say "thank you", then maybe I could leave them a present next time I collected supplies? A jar of Vegemite, perhaps? The soldiers were fond of Vegemite.

I made porridge and coffee and roused the Humans. We had a hundred and six customers who would be wanting breakfast real soon.

Drander emerged, just as the first of those customers trickled down to the dining room.

'You let me sleep,' she said with accusation in her tone.

I handed her a coffee jug. 'You needed it. We could manage.'

She opened her mouth to reply. I turned her around and gave her a gentle shove in the direction of the tables. 'Go. Serve. We need you now.'

She glared at me, but, as more customers came in, recognised I was right, and went to help Enya. I called Rita to me, and sent her into the kitchen.

The CO seemed distracted through breakfast. While his soldiers were wolfing down everything in sight and exclaiming over the exotic tastes and textures, he barely touched anything. Every few minutes his wrist phone went off.

I pointed it out to Drander and asked, 'What's happening?'

'Guess,' she replied.

My stomach did a flip flop, and I must have gone pale, because Drander reached out and drew the blood back into my cheeks. A little too much.

I caught her wrist. 'Don't. I can look after myself.'

'Sure, worm?'

I nodded, and said, 'Grub.'

She frowned.

'Your babies look like witchetty grubs, not worms.'

'Wit-che-tty,' she said carefully sounding the word out. 'What are they?'

'Up north, they grow big enough to eat. They're quite a delicacy,' I said callously and watched her grow darker, but she didn't dare bring attention to us.

She compressed her lips and got back to the tables. I felt like a cad, but a part of me got satisfaction from being able to turn the tables on our relationship.

After breakfast, the CO made an announcement. I didn't need Drander's translation to realise they were staying longer. The invasion was temporarily halted as they attempted to reconsolidate what they thought they had already won. This meant a hundred and six soldiers would remain billeted in our hotel until further notice.

'Better cancel the [General]'s booking for tomorrow night,' I said flippantly. And then added more seriously, 'And I've run out of that yellow stuff. And probably everything else by tomorrow.'

She didn't respond. She was a thousand miles away. I clicked my fingers in front of her noseless face.

'Oi. Here. Now. We need you.'

She opened her eyes wide, multiple eyelids fluttering. 'What?'

'We have a hundred and six unexpected guests. This needs dealing with in the here and now,' I said.

'Oh. Yes,' she said vaguely, but then she drew a deep breath and took control again, as I knew she would. 'Get me another staff member. Get me the list of supplies you need, I'll get it delivered. And let me handle the bookings.'

Two refugees applied. I took both. One for Drander and one for the kitchen; both ladies. One was maybe 19 or 20, and the other in her early thirties. We assigned the younger one to the kitchen as she'd worked in a fast food place before. Both had children. The kitchen one arrived with a four-year-old in tow. We didn't know about the three children the other one had until Enya spotted them hiding behind the laundry later that night and dragged them into the kitchen. Drander's colour got alarmingly dark as she surveyed the three. Stick thin Asian kids with a mop of black hair, and wide black eyes staring out of solemn little faces. At a guess, the two older ones, William and Karen, were around Rita's age, while the youngest would have barely been out of nappies.

Their mother, Jennifer she was called, gathered them fearfully to her. 'Please,' she whispered.

Drander's hand came up in a very familiar gesture.

I stepped close to Drander and whispered in her ear, 'The children are held hostage to the parent's good behaviour.'

Drander whirled and used her powers on me, kind of like stamping a foot in temper. In agony, I went into a foetal position, but she was done, and I was allowed to recover in peace.

'We don't run a nursery. They work or you all leave. That applies to all children,' Drander said to the three mothers present.

They nodded, staring at me. The worst was the look Enya gave her. I saw betrayal, shock, hurt. Enya had clearly thought they were friends. That was dead now.

Drander's face echoed Enya's pain. I think she realised what her temper tantrum had just cost her. Drooping, she left the kitchen to us Humans and went up to our room.

I straightened up, feeling like the meat in a rather nasty sandwich. I wanted to go after her, but that would alienate me from my fellow Humans. What would I do anyway? I couldn't hug her and assure her they would forgive her in time. I wasn't sure they could. Besides, I couldn't bear to be touched; had been shrugging off her attentions and avoiding Chef's camaraderie all day. I was unclean.

I stared at my feet as the silence lengthened.

'You're right, she's not your Missus, is she?' Chef asked.

I shook my head.

'She owns you,' he continued.

'She is not our enemy. Our guests are.'

'Why don't we kill them, then?' asked Sean.

'Because if you do that, Drander will be forced to kill us. She won't have a choice. If she refuses, her entire family—parents, siblings, kids—will be on the receiving end. And we will all still die.'

Their faces reflected how that changed their attitude towards her. I hoped it was enough.

'Are we safe?' whispered Jenny, clutching her children.

I could see I was going to have to buy more clothes in my copious spare time. They were as filthy as all the other refugees.

'You're safer here with Drander and me, than you are on the streets,' I said. 'Just keep the children away from the guests. They can get a bit rough. When I get a chance, I'll take the older children down to the Catholic school and enrol them.'

'We're not Catholic,' said the mother working in the kitchen with Sean and Chef. Dianne—that was her name—was far too young to be caring for a four-year-old, looking barely older than Sean. I think she was part aboriginal. The child certainly seemed so.

'Only school open,' I said. 'All the Government schools closed up shop months ago.

'That is, if you stay.' I looked at them all. 'My last staff ran away. I gave my word I wouldn't, but none of you have. You're free to go back to the streets. If you're going to do it, best you go now, though.'

They understood.

'She'll punish you, won't she?' Chef said. It wasn't really a question.

I shrugged. 'She punished me last time. I'm still alive.'

Chef sighed. 'I'm in, Ale,' he said. 'I'm much safer here than out there. I have you to thank for that.'

'I'm not leaving you,' said Sean.

I wondered what I'd done to engender such fierce loyalty, but I was glad of it.

'Then I guess we're staying too,' said his mother. 'A proper bedroom and enough sleep would be nice though.'

I had to smile at that. 'Yeah, it would, wouldn't it.'

'Aye,' said Chef, who was still sleeping on sacks in our cellar.

'When we get rid of this mob,' I said, 'you can have your pick of accommodation.'

That was acceptable to them all. There weren't a lot of real options for them, but I was glad they had chosen to stay. We got on with the business of preparing for another day with our unexpected guests.

I'd just finished cleaning the bar, when the [General]'s security officer arrived with Dr'gor and a couple of others, none of them looking happy. I offered to get Drander for them, but it was me he wanted to talk to.

'Did your master leave the hotel yesterday?' his translator asked.

'My what?' I asked.

The translator gestured to Dr'gor and themselves. 'Your—'

'Drander?' I asked.

They nodded.

'You know she didn't.'

There was some confusion at my use of the feminine pronoun, but the message got passed back accurately enough.

'Did you?'

I nodded. 'I do the shopping.'

'Last night?'

I nodded again. 'I saw him off,' I said, pointing to Dr'gor. I knew I hadn't said anything they didn't already know, but I wanted to know what else they knew, so I asked, 'What's this about?'

Apparently, I wasn't allowed to know anything because they left without another word, taking Dr'gor with them.

She was there the instant I closed the front doors. She tried to put her hands on my shoulder, but I still couldn't handle it and flinched. She contented herself with a soft 'Thank you.'

Knowing how alien that was to her, I acknowledged it with a nod and managed a fleeting smile.

There was a sound, like a 'pop' outside and she cried out. I caught her as she fell forwards. Enya opened the door and looked out, quickly shutting it again. She was white.

'They ... they shot that one you pointed to,' she said.

'Oh, God. That was Drander's batchling.' I held Drander closer, even though her body was making my skin crawl. "*Unclean*," my mind still sang. "*I am unclean.*"

'You pointed at him,' Enya said.

'They knew anyway,' I said. '[Drander's people] are tagged. They always know where they are.'

'[Yes],' whispered Drander. She sat up and moved out of my arms. 'Yes. They knew.' She stood up, unsteady on her feet, looking at all our staff. Even Chef was hovering over by the kitchen door looking concerned. 'They just wanted to be sure I hadn't found a way to get out of my tag. Pass it on to someone, or ... or something. He ... He did the right thing.'

'Why ... why would they kill your ... what did you call him? ... batchling? Does this mean they'll kill you?' Enya must have been remembering what I'd said earlier.

But Drander shook her head. 'I don't think so. I think if they were going to, they would have done it already,' she said, answering the second question only. Her eyes exhibited the same luminosity I had seen in Dr'gor's eyes. She blinked all three eyelids, and it was gone. 'Bed everyone. Tomorrow is another day.'

She meant "later today" of course, but no-one corrected her.

After breakfast later that morning, the CO announced that they were all leaving as had been scheduled the previous day. We heaved a collective sigh of relief, but wondered why. As everyone tackled the massive task of cleaning up after them, I took the trolley, and my gift, across to the ships.

At the edge of the park I saw why it was no longer deemed to be an issue. As far as the eye could see, all around the park, lay the dead.

Drander's people, all of them.

I counted fifty on our side of the park, but more stretched around the corner, and I guessed at the same number on each side. Two hundred people. One thousand babies with two parents for each batch of ten. That meant two hundred parents. Dr'gor's babies had been amongst those I killed. These must be their parents.

I stood there, looking at all those dead bodies, crying and feeling sick. *Unclean*, my mind kept saying. Twelve hundred dead because of me.

'So? What? We have dissent in the ranks, do we?' My once friend and neighbour, Ron, of the luggage shop was standing beside me. I hadn't heard him arrive. He kicked one of the dead Aliens. 'Good to see it.'

With tears in my eyes and rage in my heart, I spat out what thundered inside me. 'These ones are not our enemy. Our enemy are the crocodile people. These are all dead because one, just one of them, tried to help us Humans.'

Leaving him gaping and spluttering for a comeback, I leapt over the nearest corpse and sprinted for the ships.

My friendly ship Alien was waiting for me. It brushed the tears from my cheeks with its feathery touch and chittered. When I clearly didn't understand, it whispered 'heeeero,' at me.

I shook my head in misery.

It continued stroking me. Under the influence of that gentle pressure, I calmed down.

'War is Hell,' I told it.

'[Yes].'

I don't know if it understood the reference, but that was the right response. I remembered the Vegemite and held out the jar.

It tilted its head in query. I unscrewed the lid and scraped a little off on to my finger and held it out. Its mouth parts felt as feathery light as its "hands" upon my hand.

'Aah.'

Gravely it took the jar from me and put the lid back on. It chittered something which could only be "Thank you" and flew up the ramp.

I tasted the sound of that chitter in my mouth and resolved to pass it on to Drander. Clearly their chittering language was not the same as the crocodile people's language.

'It said what?' demanded Drander.

Carefully I repeated the chittering sounds. I was sure I had them exactly as I remembered.

She sat down gaping at me. 'What?'

I carefully repeated it chitter by chitter to be sure I had it right.

She waved her hand, 'I heard it the first time.'

'Well, what then? I thought it meant "thank you".
But you said there is no "thank you".'

'There isn't. You want to know what it really said?'

'Well, yes.'

Dianne and the Chef wanted to know too. I forget
where Sean was. Putting the rubbish out, maybe? As
the most junior he still got all the fun jobs.

'It said, literally translated, that you could lay your
eggs in its ship anytime.'

My eggs in its ship? 'Is that like a proposal of marriage
or something?'

She blew raspberries. 'No, it's more literal than that.
It offered you and your children sanctuary, if you ever
need it.'

'Sanctuary?'

She nodded. 'They'll keep you hidden from [the
General's people] should you ask them for it.'

All I could think to say, knowing why I might need
it, was "He'll kill them. All of them."

She shrugged. 'The offer is made. They will all
honour it.'

'Hive mentality,' I murmured, still reeling from the
magnitude of the offer.

'We think so. We think they are telepathically
linked to all [ship people] throughout the galaxy. But
no-one really knows. They don't talk much. I know
more about your people than I do about them.'

'Our people?' Chef asked.

She sighed and grimaced. 'Your people. I specialised
in the study of your people on the way here.'

'How long?'

She blinked. 'Since I could crawl.'

'Not you. Your ships.'

She shook her head. 'I can't measure it in your years. It makes no sense.'

He sighed. 'And I suppose if I asked you where you came from, you wouldn't be able to answer it in terms I can understand either.'

'That's easy. I was born on a ship, in transit. Where the ship came from, even if I could answer, I wouldn't.'

'But your parents are back there,' I said.

'No.' She shook her head. 'This trip was more than one generation. My parents are elsewhere on this planet.'

'This is all over the world?' asked Dianne, startled.

'Didn't you realise?' I asked.

She shook her head, making her brunette curls bounce all over her face, 'I thought ...'

'You thought you'd be able to find somewhere safe, somewhere they weren't.' Chef's tone sounded sympathetic. 'We all thought that once.'

'That's why you took to the roads in the first place, isn't it?' Drander asked.

'Yes,' said Sean and Dianne in unison.

Chef grimaced and refrained from answering.

Drander grimaced too and went out to the laundry. I'm not sure if it was because she knew when to retreat, or if she just wanted to be alone.

Being alone, even with no guests, wasn't really a possibility with five children underfoot; even if they were working as hard as the seven adults.

I grabbed Robin (Jenny's youngest boy) and Justine (Dianne's little girl) and took them for a run around the playground in the park as soon as I could. There was a really good playground across the road, but I could hardly take them through the barricade of corpses, so I took them around the corner and further away from the city to another park I knew. We couldn't stay long but we all enjoyed ourselves. Just watching them chase each other and climb and laugh was the best medicine in the world. On the way back, I stopped at the supermarket, bought them both a small chocolate, as well as some stuff for the evening's customers—The [General]'s group had confirmed their original booking. My inner voice still sang "unclean", but more softly now, and not at all when Robin asked to be picked up and Justine skipped alongside. It was the happiest hour of my life.

After lunch Jenny put them both to sleep in my bed. Not having a room of their own yet, and with every other room in the place undergoing some variation of cleansing, it was the only quiet place.

Then we took the—by now exhausted—older children down to the school. They fell asleep outside the principal's office. They looked such a peaceful sight, two black hairs framing a fair hair in identical clothing, sitting in a row, propping each other up. It seemed criminal to wake them up for their interview and entrance test. If I had known there would be one of those I would have waited until the next day and brought them in straight after breakfast and a good night's sleep. As it was, Rita ended up in the same class as Karen, who was almost a year younger than her, while William, who was a year older than Rita, went into the class above.

Initially.

Both wasted a month at this level before being promoted. In the long run a month of revision didn't hurt, but both were annoyed and determined to do better.

As the principal explained, they had to do this because they had children from all sorts of backgrounds from all over the country, all having had a gap in their schooling. They just had no other way to gauge where to put a child. But it also meant they were quite flexible about moving them. We arranged to pay weekly and took them back home, where they were allowed to join the younger children in my bed.

By the time the [General]'s party arrived, we'd sorted out the accommodation situation and the younger children had been sent to their new beds with the older children looking after them. Life settled into a pattern for a while.

On the last day of their second week at school, someone threw stones at our three after school. One stone split Karen's brow, and she arrived home sobbing and bleeding. While the Chef cleaned it up, Drander, skin darkened to an unpleasant shade, marched up to the school to speak to the principal.

'Should someone stop her?' asked Jenny.

'Nope. She won't do any permanent damage. But,' I said to the kids, 'you are about to become the most unpopular kids in school. The safest, but definitely the most unpopular.'

'At least one thing will change, then,' said Rita in a bitter tone.

'Meaning?' asked her mother.

'We were already the most unpopular,' William said.

'Why didn't you say?' Jenny attempted to hug him.

'What difference was it going to make?' Rita shrugged. 'You weren't going to let us stay home, were you?'

'Another school?' said the Chef.

'You don't get out a lot, do you?' I growled at him. 'More and more places are closing down, every day. We are lucky to have a school, especially one so close to here. Hell, I'm amazed we can still buy fresh bread.'

'Doctors?' he asked, inspecting Karen's forehead, and grimacing at the sight of the wound.

Sean and I looked at each other in consternation. I knew of none. Sean shook his head. We were the only two who left the hotel.

'Is the hospital still open?' Chef asked. There used to be a big hospital about a mile north of us.

'They shut that down in the first week of the invasion. Evacuated everyone to the country, even the doctors.' I said.

'She needs stitches.' Chef said.

I looked at the cut he'd exposed. He was right. I touched my own scar reflexively.

'There is something I can try.'

They all looked at me. 'Do you trust me?' I asked Jenny.

She looked between me and her daughter, her eyes wide.

'Is it something to do with the Aliens?' asked William.

I nodded. 'Do you trust me?' I repeated.

'I do.' Karen hopped down off the bench she'd been on and took my hand. 'Are we going to the ships, Uncle Ale?'

'Yes. Frightened?' I smiled down at her.

'Not with you.'

'Good girl.'

I carried her past the rotting corpses with her head buried in my shoulder and onwards to the supply ship. At the ship I set her down and waited. Shortly after, the entrance opened and one of those flying skeletons floated down. It folded itself into a squat and examined the cut. Karen pressed against my leg, but remained where she was, looking up at it, her big black eyes wide with fear. The creature chittered.

'I think it just said, "Don't be afraid",' I told her.

A couple of raspberries. '[Yes].'

'This will hurt,' I warned her, 'but only for a few seconds, and then everything will be fine. Okay?'

She nodded solemnly. Brave little girl that she was, she didn't even cry out when the globule hit her, although I felt her jerk.

Satisfied, it stood up again, took my chin and looked deeply into my eyes with its blind looking stare. '[Open].'

'I'm fine,' I started to say, but as soon as I opened my mouth to speak the globule landed inside, and once again I swallowed automatically.

It pressed something into my hand and flew back up into the ship. It turned out to be a piece of something like paper with alien markings which might have been writing on it. If it was writing, I couldn't read it, so I shoved it into my pocket and carried Karen back home.

'Where did this come from?' Drander hissed at me when I showed the paper to her as we prepared for bed.

'[The ship people]. What is it?'

'It's an address. With a number.'

'What sort of number?'

'Forty. Get dressed again.'

I stared at her. She couldn't mean ...?

'Forty. Four batches.'

She did mean what I thought she meant.

I groaned. 'Where is it?'

'I don't know.' She found a pen and started translating the symbols on the paper to our alphabet.

I looked at what she had written. Worked it out.

'It's about a ten-minute walk away.'

She handed me the piece of paper.

I sat holding it, my eyes closed. "*Unclean*" my mind sang. "Hero" [the ship person] had said, and they'd given me the stamina to manage it. "War is Hell" I had said, and they had agreed.

'Welcome to Hell,' I muttered, and went to find the place.

This place was guarded, but not very well. Besides I was invincible. At least that is how I felt with the Alien's saliva in my bloodstream. I was in and out in ten minutes and back home in another ten.

Drander greeted me by handing me a shot of whisky and understood when I crawled into a corner of our bathroom shaking and keening. She threw a blanket over me and went to bed.

I understood now. I had become the baby assassin. Every time they attempted to lay some batches down, I would be sent in. These babies had been much smaller than the previous babies and there'd been a lot of empty nests waiting to receive their precious burden.

I cried for the souls of the one thousand, two hundred and forty people whose death I was responsible for. I spelled the number out in my head—

in word form, not a string of digits. Each life meant more to me that way.

I cried all night, but once again numbness crept in before I had to get up and face the day amongst Humans and Aliens. And once again the globule sustained me until midnight the following day.

But there were fresh bodies in the park the next morning.

'I don't want to do this again,' I told Drander that night, in bed.

'I know,' she said, giving me a quick hug.

But, two weeks later, when a note got slipped in amongst the shopping, I didn't even tell her. I used the previous note, with Drander's translation, to work out what it said and just did it. A hundred more souls to add to the ever-growing tally. But this place was guarded by closed circuit television cameras, and one captured a partial portrait of me before I torched it.

The [General] himself put me up on the notice board. He had no idea who it was, except that it was Human. There wasn't enough to tell much more. If Drander recognised her hoodie, she said nothing. No-one else seemed to recognise me either, and I wasn't about to enlighten anyone.

A curfew was introduced. All Humans off the streets by 22:00.

How do you get off the street when you don't have a home to go to?

Every night we would hear the 'pop' of the Alien's guns going off, and the tally of souls grew. All of them a weight on my conscience. I stopped counting after a few weeks, but I still felt them.

Every night Drander and Enya would take a huge pile of sandwiches and cheese out to the unused garage behind the hotel. Every morning the food would be gone as the refugees sought a safe place off the street. At that stage it wasn't illegal to help them. That came later.

Because, you know something? When the Aliens targeted the millions of refugees and forced them to start gathering indoors at night, that's when Humans started to organise. That's when the resistance was born. Here, in this country, where the weather made sleeping outdoors possible all year round.

I did one more hit before events changed again. I couldn't get close to the babies because they were too well guarded. I was forced to torch the whole building, guards and all. I was reasonably certain I only got crocodile people, but with so many Human and Alien deaths which could be laid at my door, it didn't really matter to me any longer. I don't know how successful I was either, because I didn't hang around. Nor could you tell by heightened activity the next day. We almost permanently had a full house now, as soldiers poured in from elsewhere to quell an uprising which they just couldn't get a grip on.

They could no longer run, so people, individually and in small groups, were hitting back. But the more Humans the Aliens killed, the more Humans figured they had nothing to lose, and the more Humans joined the informal guerrilla campaign.

I still have no idea how that last hit went.

The [General] still ate at our place regularly with twenty or so of his closest staff and cronies. The last few visits I noticed Drander looking very nervous around him. She said nothing though, so I thought maybe I was imagining it.

However, one night at the coffee and port stage, he called her over and, looming over her, inspected her very closely, to the point of removing her top and examining the skin underneath. She closed two eyelids and endured it. Then he made a noise of disgust and slapped her. She was flung against a table with the strength of the hit and her nose openings started to bleed luminous stuff, like the tears, but darker. Concerned, Enya and I rushed to her.

The [General] rumbled at us. Then he frowned and beckoned me to him.

'No! [No]!' Drander grabbed for me. She pulled herself back up into a kneeling position and prostrated herself on the floor. '[No. The Hotel needs him].'

'[The Hotel needs you]. Come, Human.'

I hesitated, looking from one to the other. What was happening? If Drander didn't want this to happen, it couldn't be good.

'Come!' he bellowed, and two of his minions grabbed my arms and, lifting my feet off the ground, carried me over to him.

I had to endure the same inspection. He kept tapping my scarred cheek as well. Then he nodded and started to undo the fastenings on his trousers.

That was enough for me. Whatever it was, I wanted no part of it. I no longer cared if this unclean murdering body I inhabited lived or died. I fought, I bit, I yelled. And as a large tube came from his nether regions, I ducked and weaved my head every which way to avoid it. Someone hit me—hard.

I came to in the middle of the night, lying on my back in my bed. My stomach and my lips hurt, but other than that I seemed to be fine.

Normally Drander and I slept with our backs together, facing away from each other, but tonight she had an arm draped over my chest. I reached up to remove it and discovered a catheter in the back of my right hand. I followed the tube attached to me to find a drip on a stand.

I moved my left arm to try to remove the drip, and she tightened her arm against me, effectively pinning that arm.

'Don't,' she said. 'You need it.'

I turned my head to look at her. Tears formed at the base of her eyes.

I opened my mouth to speak and discovered I couldn't.

Touching my mouth, I felt … stitches.

I threw her arm off me and propped myself on my elbow, glaring at her. *What the hell was going on?* I wanted an explanation, and I wanted it now.

'It should have been me,' she said.

That wasn't an explanation.

'I've been working too hard, and I haven't been eating enough. I didn't put on enough weight. I'm sorry.'

Okay. That's an apology for something else. Where's the explanation?

A tear fell from an eye.

'You're pregnant.'

Idiotically, my brain kept saying, *That's not possible. I shoot blanks.* I even tried to utter the words.

But, of course, it wasn't my sperm that had created this. And then, *But I don't have a womb* and then the reason why my mouth might be sewn shut and why there was a pain in my stomach became obvious. I started to scrabble at my mouth, intent on ripping out the stitches, as I felt bile rise, but she yanked my hand away.

'Don't. Don't make me restrain you. Please.'

She pointed to the end of our bed to a strange circular contraption about seven feet in diameter. In the dark I couldn't make out much else.

I pulled my hand away from her. She let me, probably fearful of dislodging the catheter.

This couldn't be. It wasn't possible. It was just sooo wrong! I pounded the bed with my fist, and she moved out of the way.

"Help me!" I wanted to cry out.

Another tear rolled out, this time from her other eye. 'I told you I was a <something>. It means that I was meant to carry the [General]'s baby during its second phase.'

Yes, you! Why me? I hit the bed in frustration again, hoping my actions asked the question.

She touched my scar. 'When [the ship person] did that, they marked you as a compatible carrier. With you Humans able to do that, my kind are no longer necessary.'

Did this make her happy, or sad? I couldn't tell.

I fell back, staring dry-eyed at the ceiling. My mind still kept telling me it hadn't happened. I would wake up in the morning and discover it was all a nightmare.

But the morning light came, and nothing had changed.

Drander had finally slept as the night started turning to grey. I watched as the contraption at the foot of the bed turned from a circular silhouette to a wire frame about two feet deep. I gently disengaged her arm and slipped from the bed. She slept on as I examined the device. On one side of the circle there was a human shaped indentation with straps down one side of each limb and the body. Down one edge were metal hooks, obviously meant to hold bags like catheter currently attached to me. The frame could be swung in almost any direction.

"Don't make me restrain you," she had said. Anyone put in this contraption would be totally immobilised.

You can't. You wouldn't, I pleaded silently. But she would. If she was ordered to do it, she would. She could no more disobey orders than stop breathing.

Trembling, I staggered away from it, and into the bathroom. I was so weak I collapsed onto the toilet and sat there for a long time.

When I could, I pulled myself up and looked in the mirror. My lips were welded shut by a thin dark green line of the same waxy substance as had been put on Karen's and my cuts. Then over the top of that a dark coloured thread had been used to sew them closed as well.

I started hunting through the drawers for a pair of scissors.

'[No].'

Drander stood in the doorway, swaying with fatigue, grey rather than green, the first eyelid almost completely down, and yawning. But there. Ready to stop me.

I sat on the edge of the bath and glared at her.

'I'm sorry,' she said hoarsely and refused to look me in the eye. 'Come back to bed.'

I thumped the bath and refused to move.

'Please, don't,' she murmured, leaning against the door jamb, second eyelid joining the first.

What have you done to me? I wanted it undone. Now.

'Come back to bed. Please,' she asked, pulling herself up and holding her hand out to me.

I contemplated refusing again, but we were both tired, and I knew she could enforce it. I stood up. Too quickly. My stomach tried to leave via my mouth, and I found myself gagging.

'Don't. Don't. It will burn you.'

She held me upright by sheer force.

Still holding me upright, she dragged me and my drip back into the bedroom. I'd never realised before how strong she was. She let go of me with one hand to hunt through the mess on the bedside table, found what she was after, and held up a needle.

I started to back away, but she shook her head. '[No]. [It will help]. Stay still. Very still. I have to find your ...' Whatever it was, she found it, and jabbed me. My stomach settled instantly.

She massaged the needle's entry point and looked me in the eyes again. 'The baby is in your stomach. It needs an acidic environment. Your stomach has been prepared for that. Your ...' She gestured up and down her front in a vertical motion.

Oesophagus, I guessed.

'That part of you has not. It is not good for you, or the baby, to try to get rid of it too early. It is too acidic. It will burn as it comes up.'

I touched my lips, pushing against the green stuff.

'When the baby is ready, that will be absorbed, preparing the way.'

I touched the stitches on top of the wax.

'That's to stop it leaving until we get you to a proper receptacle.'

I didn't want to know anymore. I didn't want to hear it. This just wasn't happening to me.

I sat as a wave of dizziness swept over me. She took control and settled my blood back into its proper distribution. Now I knew why her people had that power. She felt my forehead like a mother taking a child's temperature, and I realised why the other ability existed too. It was almost time to get up, but I wasn't sorry when she switched the alarm off and put me back in bed, before climbing in herself. Despite having the mother of all heartburn, I slept.

I found out later that whatever was in that needle, it would have this affect on me every time. Over time I built up some resistance, in so far as it would take longer to work, and work for a shorter period of time, but I still crashed for hours each time.

Several hours later she helped me dress and half carried me down to the kitchen. Everyone was busy with their respective jobs, so only the Chef was in there. That was the first time I heard "Nil by Mouth" and "pregnant" in relation to me. I couldn't bear to face his pity, so I sat looking at the floor while Drander drank coffee and nibbled on that purple stuff.

Brunch over, she escorted me into the bar. And briefly left me.

Someone had left a mess serving the morning drinks. This offended my sense of rightness, so I found a clean cloth and started work. I was so tired and weak that I had to keep sitting and resting, but I had the bar ready for opening an hour before lunch; the time our guests usually started trickling in from whatever marauding party they'd been assigned to. I managed the lunch rush, but I was so exhausted by the end of lunch that Drander had a trundle bed set up in the kitchen for me.

Robin and Justine collectively stamped their feet and demanded to be allowed to have their nap with me. Robin tucked down and went to sleep immediately with a contented little sigh, but Justine kept wriggling and trying to chat with me. I was too tired to respond, and eventually Dianne gave up and took her, crying, to her own bed. It was a hard lesson for a little child, but she learnt it. After she left, I slept with one arm holding Robin close for our mutual comfort.

Drander called all the staff to her when the children got home from school and explained the situation. "Nil by mouth", "pregnant" and "watch like a hawk" I heard. *Why?*

'If he does anything to lose the baby, WE are ALL dead. All of us.' Drander had included herself in that comment.

'Like attempt to off himself?' Chef asked shrewdly.

Drander needed a translation, but having received it, agreed.

Brave little Karen appointed herself my first guardian, and fell asleep across my legs, "watching like a hawk". At some stage Justine defied her mother and crept back.

I woke up, unable to move for the number of little bodies pressed around me, and Drander standing over me, a curious smile on her lips and that "two eyelids half down" look.

During dinner, my movements were so slow Enya left off waiting tables and came to help me. I sat by the computer and showed her where and what while she did the actual serving. She apologised for eating her tea in front of me, but I didn't care. My stomach hurt and I had no appetite anyway. I was glad when we closed the bar and Drander led me back upstairs. She gave me the injection again and put me to bed.

I mimed teeth cleaning, and she snorted. 'You'll be lucky to have teeth to worry about when this is over,' she said and bared her own perfect set.

I endured this for over a week.

During the weekend I had had a constant shadow in the form of one or another or all the children except when in the bar. That was off-limits to them. While I resented the constant guard, I couldn't be angry with the children. They were trying to help. We played "snap" and "old maid" and I helped with their homework when I wasn't actively working the bar. Then the older three went back to school, and I found myself counting the minutes until they got home each day.

By Wednesday of the second week, I'd had enough.

They left me alone to do the morning stocktake while they were busy with the linen changeover. Drander gave me a puzzled look as she followed Jenny up the stairs. I heard her suggest to Jenny that Robin could play with me and heard Jenny's refusal.

Then I was alone.

I did my usual checks, made my list, and made my way down to the cellar. I was so weak that I had to wait at the bottom of the stairs for the trembling to cease. We used a wheelbarrow to collect the bottles I wanted upstairs or near the stairs during the evening and I leant heavily on this as I made my way to my desk. It was just a side table with a single drawer in it. I used it to rest bottles on while they breathed, and other bits and pieces.

Today, I put down the list and pulled a pair of scissors out of the drawer.

When I'd come downstairs this morning, I had been so clear in my mind about what to do, but now, I was no longer sure. I was killing yet another baby. Somehow it was different being my own baby, so to speak. But I only had a few minutes. Drander always knew. She already suspected. Failure was not an option. It was now or never.

I cut through the stiches and grabbed one end of
the seal and pulled. I cried out as I pulled a layer of
skin away with it When I opened my mouth and took a
deep breath, my stomach contents rushed up. I
couldn't stop them. And they burnt. Burnt my
oesophagus; burnt my mouth, my tongue, and my
bleeding lips. And there on the floor, in a puddle of
green liquid, was a mammalian foetus. I fell to the
floor on my hands and knees still vomiting. A dark
green spongy stuff followed.

'What have you done?' I heard someone screaming.
'Help me.'

Two people grabbed me and hauled me up the
stairs where I was thrown on my back across three
chairs hastily assembled in a line.

Still vomiting, I rolled over to face the floor and let
it out.

'Get everyone, even Chef,' I heard. 'Now, Enya! I
don't know how much time we have.'

Drander was there beside me. '[Oh, worm. Do you
even begin to understand what you have done]?' she
murmured to me, holding my hand.

The staff assembled. I heard various exclamations.
And Robin asking to be allowed to join me. Justine
asked her mother why my sick was green.

I twisted slightly so I could see them. Mostly I could
see Drander's restraining hands, one for me, one for
them.

'Pack!' she said. 'Get out of here. Run. As far away,
and as fast as you can.'

'Hide?' asked Chef.

Drander shook her head. 'You are his family. They will come looking for you. I'll give you half an hour before I report it, but I can't leave it too long, or they'll know.'

They stood silent, staring.

'Move!'

They didn't move. It wasn't her they were staring at.

'Stay.'

She whirled around and prostrated herself in front of the [General].

He—or should I think of the [General] as "she" now?—was looking at me. I had been spat at by experts in the last few months, so I saw it coming, caught it on my lips and expelled it again, unswallowed.

'[Suit yourself].' His/Her ears twitched, their version of a shrug.

I decided "his" was as good a possessive pronoun as any.

I was sorry for not accepting the globule already. Wherever his spit had touched, the pain was gone. Everything else, from my stomach upwards, was still burning, and I was still expelling a green slime.

'[There's something to be said for <something>],' he mused, kicking Drander. '[A weakness Humans and your kind share. But he lasted longer than any other Human we have tried].'

I had? There were others? I hadn't lasted a fortnight. How long had they?

'[Which one of you]?' he mused, looking across at my staff. Then his eyes narrowed, and he stepped over Drander and lifted Chef up by his shirt front.

He easily carried him in this way over to the notice board and then the [General] started looking. He wouldn't find it. I had removed the notice weeks ago.

But he did find something else.

He put the Chef down and brought the partial picture of me in Drander's hoodie over.

I realised, looking up at him, that the angle of the camera and his angle of looking down at me were very similar. He hauled me up by my shirt front and held me dangling off the floor. I was still oozing slime. He ignored that and held the picture up for me to see. I fleetingly thought of denying it, but I could see in his eyes that he knew.

I hadn't thought I had anything else left to lose. I was wrong. I had everything to lose.

'[They know nothing].' I spoke carefully, making sure I had it right.

'You had help.'

'[You killed him].'

'[?]'

'Dr'gor.' I waved my arm back towards Drander and the others. '[They know nothing].'

He held up the notice and indicated Sean. 'Who is this?'

Sean went pale and bobbed his head as he answered, 'I d ... don't know, S ... Sir.'

'You will suffer,' the [General] said slowly.

I just looked him in the eye. Part of me felt glad that I would be cleansed at last.

He trod on Drander's hand and she sat up, holding it close, but still looking down.

'[Up].'

Reluctantly she stood.

'[Punish them].'

She looked at him in despair, the luminous green shimmering at the base of her eyes. I thought for a second she might refuse, but the habit of obedience is instilled in them before they leave the nests. The consequences made all too clear as soon as they reach sentience. She nodded, blinked, and cleared the green stuff. Her face had gone as stiff as the [General]'s, and her eyes were as dead.

Then, not even looking at them, she moved her hands and they all screamed. All except the Chef who had snuck back to the kitchen when he was put down by the notice board.

'Again.'

She bowed her head and moved her hand again. Once more they all screamed. Justine didn't stop. And Robin; Robin hung limp in his mother's arms.

'Again.'

'[No],' I implored in their language before switching back to English.

'No more. They are not responsible.' *Not my Robin.* 'I'll do anything. Just leave them alone.' *Please, God, let Robin be all right.* I was still being held up, and I met the [General]'s eyes with mine.

79

'I promise,' I whispered.

'[Anything]? Anything?'

I nodded. Trembling.

'You will regret.'

I nodded, dropping my eyes at last. '[I know].'

He dropped me. I needed Drander's help to stay upright.

'Come.'

He strode for the door. I couldn't walk that far or that fast. At the door he realised this and gestured for one of his soldiers to pick me up and carry me.

I heard him telling someone, '[Tag them].'

For the next two weeks he kept me close by him. When I couldn't keep up, I was carried. I learnt to eat their food. It was either that or starve, and he wouldn't let me starve. He had some purple stuff reduced to a slush and forced it down my throat. I gagged and coughed, but it mostly stayed down. At night I slept on the floor of his room, as far away from him as I could get. He hardly ever acknowledged me, but he noticed when I didn't eat, when I tried to slip away, or failed to keep up with his hectic schedule.

His staff treated me as some sort of pet, something to take out their feelings towards the [General] on. I was kicked, I was thumped, I had food stolen from me, and they called me names, and taunted my Human weaknesses, but they stopped short of any real damage. I kept my head down and spoke not at all.

Only the [General] knew I could understand most of what was going on around me, and he didn't care.

On the two nights in those two weeks when he and his people dined at the hotel, Drander fed me my favourite Human foods, and I touched her hand in thanks, but the [General] growled when I tried to speak with her. I kept my head down and ignored all my former colleagues and friends.

After two weeks he had one of those circular contraptions brought into his War room, where he spent large portions of most days following his campaign of conquest. He beckoned, and I allowed him to pick me up and place me in the hollows. He adjusted things so my feet were flat on the base, my crotch just clear of the juncture of the leg hollows, and the arm hollows coming at right angles from the body at the correct point. He caressed my cheek, looking down at me. The angle of the head hollow meant I could look up at him. I did so, giving nothing away. He sighed, and strapped me in. Then he swung it around so that my head was level with his crotch.

I knew what was coming, but couldn't move, and no-one was kind enough to knock me out this time. The best I could manage was to close my eyes and endure as the next foetus was deposited, and my lips were resealed.

Then he swung the contraption back upright and had it positioned where he could see me constantly. A final strap went across my mouth for good measure.

It was only a matter of hours before it became unbearable. I could move just enough to change my weight from my feet to my crotch, but that pulled my arms up, and I could only bear the weight there for a short time before being forced to put the weight back onto my feet. By the second day the blood was beginning to pool in my feet, and they began to swell. My neck hurt from the odd angle it was being held at. I tried some isomeric exercises to get the blood flowing and keep muscle tone.

On the third day, Drander was admitted into the War room. I almost wept for joy at the sight of her. She avoided looking at anything as they brought her over. She placed her hand on me and sent the blood singing through my veins; got the swelling down and my heart pumping strongly again. I almost felt good again. She told them I was dehydrated and needed more liquid; suggested I be put horizontal for a few hours a day.

Then she finally looked me in the eyes and said, 'Everyone is tagged now, even Chef. They haven't hurt us though.'

I blinked to let her know I understood. Robin?

She sighed. 'This is so much easier with my people. There are a dozen things we can say with our eyelids. There is only one thing you can say with yours.'

I blinked rapidly.

'All right, two.'

Slow blink.

The [General] rumbled.

She sighed and leant forward to kiss my forehead. 'I'll be back when I'm allowed, worm.'

Slow blink.

I did cry, real tears, as she was hustled from the room and away from me.

The [General] looked from one of us to the other and saw something about us. He appeared puzzled, but I could see him working things out. What, I didn't know, but we had definitely given him something to think about. Over the next few weeks he asked that all situations where Drander's people had been placed in charge of Humans be reviewed.

When no-one else was in the room, he ruminated aloud on the phenomena he was mapping. On all the other planets they had control of he'd never encountered the Human propensity to distinguish between the types. Never encountered our tolerance and willingness to understand our "owners". We had a name for it—Stockholm Syndrome. When someone has absolute power over you, you will do anything to make them happy. Their enemy becomes your enemy. And all over the globe, [Drander's people] were recruiting Humans to their cause and it wasn't all one way. Drander wasn't the only one who was forming personal friendships with those they were supposed to control. While no-one would admit it, it was obvious from the reports the [General] was receiving, she wasn't the only one helping us, either.

'[But why],' he would shout, '[are you killing their hatchlings if you love them so much]?'

So, the campaign to prevent another hostage generation was continuing, was it?

I couldn't answer, of course, but the more I heard, the less unclean I felt. And with nothing else to do, I was absorbing everything I heard and saw in that room. No-one, not even Drander, knew I could read their language as well as understand it.

Time moved on. Drander visited every few days, and each time reported the doings of our little family. 'Sean is eighteen. He celebrated by going into the bar and getting drunk.'

On another occasion she said, 'William got Dux of the junior school. Rita is annoyed because she only got Dux of her class.' Another time she said, 'Rita has turned 9. That makes her the same age as William for about two months.'

On some other visit Drander said, 'Justine is now 5. She starts school soon.'

Shortly after she told me, 'Justine started school on Monday.' I had no idea which day had been Monday. 'She loves it.'

In one of her later offerings, Drander said, 'Enya caught Sean and Dianne kissing in the coal cellar. She's furious. But they don't exactly have anyone else, do they?'

I wondered why it had taken so long, and whether it was still possible for them to get anything like condoms.

But Robin? Months dragged by and she never mentioned him, and I couldn't ask.

Finally, the day came when the wax stuff just seemed to melt and I swallowed it. The wax felt soft and silky smooth as it slid down, cooling the heartburn I'd been living with for so long. After removing the stitches, they swung the contraption upside down. I started vomiting and regurgitated a live baby into a tub of water. Apart from the colouring, it looked very much like a human girl child. It swam about, thoroughly enjoying its freedom. I felt a surge of joy watching the precious little one. Then I expelled some spongy stuff and it was detached and taken out of the water, out of view. I heard its cry of rage and echoed the sentiment.

Then I heard the sound of the little one being slapped until it stopped crying. I could do nothing to help it. I wanted to cry with it but had no tears.

When I finished vomiting, they swung me back up and deposited the next foetus.

This one belonged to one of the [General]'s aides. He had me transferred to a nursery where they stored and "cared" for other carriers. The carers were Drander's people, as were the other carriers, and clearly, they resented me. They did what had to be done to keep me alive, but nothing more. If they had dared, they would have ignored me completely and let me starve to death, but the [General] continued to visit and check my progress, as did the "mother" of the foetus I was carrying.

In the ward we were completely isolated. I had no idea how the war was going, and no way of asking. The carers talked amongst themselves and to the other carriers, but fairly mundane matters mostly, although the occasional mention of another failed batch did come up. With nothing else to do, I spent a lot of time with my memories, especially of that perfect day when I had taken Robin and Justine to the park. *If there is a God*, I prayed, *please make Robin be okay*. I hoped he was turning four and as time went on, that he was preparing to start school.

Eventually the current baby was born and, like all crocodile people babies, received the same harsh welcome to the world.

As they swung me back up, the [General] was preparing to deposit another foetus.

'Drander?' I croaked in the few seconds I had.

He paused, frowning. '[What about it]?'

'[I haven't seen her since I came here. May I see her]?'

He opened his eyes wide in surprise, but nature took over and I had to open my mouth and receive. Talking wouldn't be possible again for months.

The [General] spoke to the head carer, who informed him that one of Drander's people had indeed tried to visit me when I first arrived, but with the policy of no outside visits, she'd been denied. He spoke angrily about having given permission for this to occur. They pulled medical rank and told him it was not good for the carriers to be disturbed by outside matters, and if he wanted his baby cared for, they knew best. He did want his baby cared for. Of course, he did.

He stopped by me before he left. '[It won't be happening].'

I hadn't cried in months. I was so chronically dehydrated, I couldn't. I buried myself in my memories again; every second of every visit she had made, revisited over and over again. Every detail of the War room puzzled out and deciphered, and as time progressed and the [General] became my only diversion, every second of his visits too.

A series of loud explosions preceded Humans bursting into our ward shooting at everything in sight. Someone in a weird mix of casual and combats, pointed a gun at me. I think they were female but couldn't remember how to tell.

[Yes], I thought, and blinked slowly as I considered blessed release.

Her jaw dropped. 'Hey, Sarge. This one's Human.'

'Get it out of there.'

She undid the straps and tried to pull me out. I couldn't help her. My muscles refused to obey. It had been a very long time since I'd remembered to exercise them. Then she had the brilliant idea of swinging the contraption upside down, and I fell flat on the floor.

'Bring him.'

She tried a fireman's lift, but my back wouldn't bend, and it was agony when she tried. Someone grabbed a door and tied me to it. Then they brought me here, wherever here is, and dumped me on the ground.

And now they are talking about me as though I don't exist. I'm used to that.

And, yes, I think I would like to live. I'm just not sure how. I want to know. If Robin is dead, I can handle that. I just want to know.

When another Human head poked itself into my view again, I gave them a long slow blink.

'Shit,' they said, and disappeared from view again.

This time several people bundled me onto a stretcher and took me into a large room with a pool in the middle. I was stripped by the simple expedient of having the clothes ripped off me and handed down to someone in the pool. I expected cold but the water was warm. Then someone else joined us. This someone appeared to be a physiotherapist because they started massaging my joints and trying to get them to bend. Eventually they shook their head.

'I can't do anything more. I need X-rays. Put him to bed.'

I was pulled out of the water, dried, and wrapped in blankets before being moved to a dormitory. My arms stuck out at right angles and bumped painfully into everything on the way, but we eventually got there.

Someone else in what looked like a Human nurse's uniform came along and removed the catheter in my hand, replacing it with another of a different design. They gave me a needle through the catheter. I tried to protest, but it took too much effort. They stuck a drip into it, muttering about why they were bothering to revive a corpse.

And another Human answered, 'Because he's carrying one of their babies. We want the baby.'

'And how many of these d'ya think I've got?' snapped the Nurse beside me, tapping the bag. By this time, I was pretty certain I had identified the Nurse as male, but couldn't see the other Human, so had no idea about them.

'I don't know. See if you can get a straw in him.'

What part of "nil by mouth" didn't the other person understand?

The man beside me sighed, and muttered, 'I'm just a nurse, not a miracle worker,' and then to me, 'Can you at least get your hands out of the way, Mate?' I screamed as he tried to bend my arms towards my side.

'Whoa, sorry. Maybe you are alive!'

I glared at him, or tried to.

He laughed at whatever face it was I achieved.

I blinked at him and tried to smile back.

'That's better. Lessee what you can do. Can you nod?'

I screwed my eyes up at the pain when I tried.

'Shake your head?'

It hurt but I found I could do that.

'Wriggle your fingers?'

And he patiently went through every muscle group in my body. Then he patted me on the shoulder and told me to keep working at it.

He came back a few minutes later with a cheap zippered jacket. He slipped one arm on and then tugged the rest under me to the other side, slipping the other arm on with some difficulty. It was far too big for me, and when both arms were inside, bunched up uncomfortably under me. He tugged until he got all the bunching on one side, and that felt better.

'Keep you warm,' he said, patting me again.

All through the long night, I tried every muscle group again, and again, and by morning I could move as long as none of my major bones were involved. But I was utterly knackered, and they had plans for me. First, they sponge bathed me. Then they X-rayed various parts of my body, then they sent me back to the physio, who pulled some extraordinary faces as she went through the X-rays. She hooked me up to some ultrasound device and for the next couple of hours moved it around my body. I dozed off during that. She massaged me for ages. The massage hurt and I really did not feel comfortable being touched like that. My nostrils flared and I frowned and whimpered, but she was relentless, or ignoring me, or both.

Then I was put back to bed, hooked up to another bag, and finally allowed to sleep. A doctor woke me up some time later and conferred with my nurse.

'What do we call you?' he asked.

I snorted and rolled my eyes at the preposterousness of the thought that I could actually answer that.

My nurse laughed. 'Starts with? Blink when I get to the right letter.'

I frowned as he went through the Human alphabet. What was my name anyway? The last thing anyone had called me was [worm], and that wasn't a name. Nor was it spelt using a human alphabet.

Patiently, he tried again, 'A?'

I blinked.

'Really? A?'

I blinked again and smiled.

'Okay. Do we get a second letter?'

I blinked again when he got to "L".

'Okay. "Al" it is.'

I blinked my acceptance. It was as good a name as any.

My nurse was "Bill" and the doctor was "Dr Dayne". I filed the information away for a time when it might be useful.

My physiotherapist had just got to the stage where she could bend one of my arms against my side when the leader of this little band of resistance fighters dropped in for a chat with me. It was a tad one-sided and full of how he was going to hold me and the baby to ransom.

That sounded awfully like he was going to sell me back to them. I had other ideas, but couldn't see any point in enlightening him, even if I could. We both agreed I had to get well first. I smiled when he said that, and he left thinking we were in accord. I wondered how much time I really had. I needed to be well for my plans to work. If he thought about it, he would realise I did not need to be well for his plans to work.

I took my first tentative steps with a walker a week later. A fortnight later I abandoned it. I was slow, every joint in my body seemed to have arthritis, but I was mobile again. I stole a pair of scissors and hid them under my mattress.

That same day they asked me to write my details down. I did, then wondered why they passed the piece of paper around, and eventually someone took it away and I was given another piece of paper.

'This time in English, please.'

I stared at the piece of paper in puzzlement. I couldn't remember how. What did an "Ale" look like?

The hospital administrator took back the piece of paper and wrote the alphabet in uppercase at the top.

I bobbed my head in gratitude and wrote "ALE, Publican, North Melbourne, born" and the date. It got easier as I went, and I remembered how to write numbers without help.

'Ale?'

I nodded.

'Um, that's not your real name surely?'

I frowned at the administrator. *Wasn't it? Why not?*

Then people burst in, all excited, and demanded that I come across to the main camp. So, I got bundled into a wheel chair and taken across the camp to the leader. He waved my first piece of paper in my face and demanded if I could read and speak Alien.

I had no idea what he was talking about, but he seemed to want agreement, so I nodded.

He handed me another piece of paper. Now I understood. I wrote "shopping list" in Human script across the top, because that's what it was.

'Shopping for what?' he wanted to know. 'Guns, ammo?'

I snorted at him and wrote "Food".

He was sooo disappointed.

'What kind of food?'

So, I rolled my eyes at him and wrote down what each item was. Stuff like rice and potatoes; the sort of stuff Drander might have ordered for our hotel. I don't know to what lengths someone had gone to to get the list, but it certainly had no military implications as far as I could tell. And this much effort was making my hand hurt. I started massaging my fingers. He noticed and sent me back to the field hospital, but I recognised the look on his face as I left. It was Drander's two eyelid look.

When I got back, I found I'd been ordered out of the dormitory and into a private room. My old bed, with the scissors under it, was already in use. I would just have to try again.

"Intelligence" sent another two notes over the next day for me to translate. Again, nothing of militaristic importance, at least not that I could discern. I stole another pair of scissors, and Bill came and turned my mattress up, shaking his head at me as he retrieved them.

I wiggled my ears, then remembered to use a shrug. *C'est la vie.*

'You don't act like the suiciders,' he said that evening as he changed my drip, 'so why are you stealing sharp objects?'

I touched my stitches.

'Oh'—he looked troubled at me—'I can't let you do that. We have orders.'

I mimed writing, and he gave me his pad and pen. I wrote slowly. I was getting better at English, but it still didn't feel natural. 'Soon. Stitches must be cut within minutes of [wax] melting.'

And indeed, I was close. And too soon. I had no way of judging time elapsed, but it just felt wrong. After two successful "births", I recognised the way the wax was softening.

'Every nurse carries a pair of scissors. Except, that is, those who are foolish enough to put theirs down near you.' He grinned as he went out.

He must have said something to someone because Dr Dayne visited, wanting to know what to do, what to feed it, that sort of thing. I could write down the birth process but had no idea what happened after that. A large tub was placed in the nearest bathroom. I saw it when I showered the next morning.

That day brought the leader back, exhorting me to hang onto the babe as long as possible. At least he had stopped talking about selling me to the highest bidder.

And that night it was all moot anyway. The wax melted about three in the morning. I leapt out of bed screaming for a nurse and staggered for the bathroom. Bill arrived, hastily shrugging on his uniform, as the first black stuff started seeping past the stitches.

I know it burnt his fingers as he struggled to cut through the tough thread, but I couldn't stop it coming. Impatiently I yanked the last few threads free.

My lips free at last, I ejected a small lifeless black lump into the tub. No bronze coloured baby swimming free. No little mammalian creature enjoying life for those brief moments before it was taught to "behave".

I picked it up in horror, still vomiting gunk.

'[No], [No].' I moaned, cradling its impossibly still, perfect form to me.

I cried and rocked and swore (in Alien) at anyone who tried to get near me.

Eventually Bill crept near me, holding a glass of milk in one bandaged hand, and a needle in the other. I chose the milk but got the needle as well anyway. As I slipped under, I held out the creature. '[Baby].' I moaned.

'We'll take care of it,' he promised.

He was as good as his word. When I woke up, with a drip still attached, I found a small parcel wrapped in a face washer and packing tape beside my bed. I took it in my arms and cradled it, falling asleep again, dreaming of Robin and Justine and brave little Karen.

They let me bury it in the hospital graveyard and gave me privacy to say a few words. I told it about its mighty Dad/Mum and its other siblings and told it to look out for them and prepare the way. Then, because it was my culture to do so, I crossed myself and murmured, 'Requiescat in Pace.'

And walked away.

Shortly after, I was discharged from the hospital and moved into the crowded crew quarters, taking up a full-time position in 'Intelligence' as a translator. I now had a personal trainer and was expected to spend each spare waking moment of every day in the small, under-resourced and overcrowded gym in some attempt to rebuild my debilitated body.

I still felt uncomfortable with so many people around me, and, after a week, stopped going.

Doctor's orders, I was told, and was escorted back at a set time every day. I was overtly supervised as I did my workout, so couldn't hide in a corner away from all the busy noisy Humans. I felt the same about the mess hall and stayed only long enough to get my food, preferring to take it elsewhere to eat.

Eating was another thing which was painful. Drander had been right about that as well. The acid had eaten away at the enamel, and now my teeth were riddled with cavities. I cleaned them as best I could, but the damage had been done and redone with each successive birth.

After a week of this, I sought out Dr Dayne and showed him my mouth.

'Shiiit. I'm no dentist, Mr Ale, and I don't think we have one in camp. I can probably remove them for you, but I can't replace them. Best to leave them where they are for the moment.'

He gave me an analgesic gel used on babies when they cut their teeth and told me he would try to find a dentist for me, or at least a dental technician, but for the moment, there was nothing he could do.

The gel helped.

One day during one of those forced workout sessions, someone came too close too fast in the gym and I reacted violently. I knew just where to hit to cause a lot of pain but no discernible damage; the [General]'s staff had taught me well.

As well as the gym, I was now ordered to see the overworked psychologist twice a week.

He asked questions in English, I replied in Alien, if at all. I could stare down the most penetrating of stares. *What could he do to me? He was nothing.* And he had better things to do than waste time with someone who didn't want help, so he discharged me after three sessions, suggesting a comprehensive review in three months.

After that, they left me alone.

I got up early and grabbed food just as the kitchen opened in the morning. Took it to my desk to eat. Stayed there until the canteen was almost closed. Grabbed some more food and scampered back to my room. Stayed there until it was time to grab food again. Sometimes, when I couldn't sleep, I would go for long walks around the camp in the middle of the night.

As I went past the hospital about two in the morning one day, someone called my name.

'Bill,' I said, placing the face.

Human faces still looked strange to me. I had gotten used to the five of them in "Intelligence", but everyone else just looked "Human" to me.

'Yeah,' he said, smiling and patting a spot on the fence beside him. 'Whatcha up to?'

'[Couldn't sleep].'

'Hey,' he said. 'Language. Try English.'

I blew raspberries. 'Sorry. Feels a bit odd still.'

'Well, I don't speak their language, so if you wanna talk, it has to be English. How long were you with them, anyway?'

I had worked this out as soon as I found out the date. 'About two and a half years.' Robin would be in his first year of school. Probably wouldn't even remember me anymore.

'Long time, not seeing a friendly face.'

'I had a friend. Two friends,' I said, realising the truth.

Was it Stockholm Syndrome or was it genuine? The two "friends" were Drander and the [General]. My "Master" and my "Captor". But they had both cared about me, in their own unique way. She called me "[worm]" as a term of endearment and tried to protect me. She had kept me healthy and let me "own" the lucrative portion of my pub. And he, despite his very busy schedule, had continued visiting me even when I wasn't carrying his baby. He had ordered that Drander be allowed to visit me also, even if his orders hadn't been obeyed. And he hadn't made my staff suffer. The [General] had left them alone when all wisdom dictated that he make an object lesson out of them— and Drander. Didn't that denote friendship?

Bill offered me a cigarette. I didn't smoke. Never had. Wasn't interested in trying either. He puffed away as I grappled with the realisation that my two best friends were Aliens. And then there was [the ship person]. Another Alien. "You may lay your eggs in my ship," it had said. "They will all honour it," Drander had said.

'Three friends,' I said, and started to cry.

He patted my shoulder, and puffed away, and let me cry.

'What's your real name?' he asked, when I finally ran out of tears and just stared into the dark. 'I don't remember. I have remembered that it isn't "Ale" though. I just don't remember anything before

Drander.' I wiped my nose on the back of my hand. He handed me a tissue and I blew. And stared, blinking in surprise. Shouldn't it have been luminous? And green?

I threw the tissue in the nearest bin.

'Kind of an appropriate name for a publican though.'

I smiled. 'Yeah.'

I looked at my stick thin hands. 'You know I used to be fat? "Stocky", I think was the polite word.'

'I know,' he said. 'The clothes they took off you were about twenty sizes bigger than you are now.'

'What happened to them?'

'Probably burnt. There was almost nothing left of them, especially at the back.'

'Pockets?'

'They found a piece of paper. A wanted notice for "The Baby Assassin".' He looked sideways at me as he said it.

I nodded. 'You got it translated, huh?' Even that felt like a different life. 'Shouldn't you be working?' I asked.

'One of the beauties about working around the clock is that if you really want to take an hour off, no-one stops you,' he said, stubbing out his cigarette.

'An hour?' I blinked at him.

'Longer,' he said with a chuckle.

'I'm sorry. I didn't mean ...'

'Don' worry about it. I like a friendly face too. You still doing gym?'

'Supposed to. They've stopped escorting me there, so ... no.'

'I'm usually there about five.'

'In the afternoon?'

'Nope. In about an hour's time.'

I yawned. 'Not tonight.' But it was useful to know. He nodded and we parted.

A couple of nights later I woke earlier than normal and decided to check it out. I didn't feel like working out—I never did—but I was feeling lonely. It was about five thirty when I got there and there were about thirty people in the gym. A large noisy crowd, all together. I started backing out again, but Bill spotted me and called me over. I hesitated, then recognised Dr Dayne and another nurse. Bill dragged me amongst them and started making the introductions.

This was the permanent staff of the hospital. Not the specialists like the psychologist or the physiotherapist. They only worked days. These were the people who were available all the time. They worked hard and obviously worked out hard as well.

It seemed natural to just go across to the hospital canteen and have breakfast with them after that. I commented as I sat down at Bill's table how friendly everyone seemed.

'What, they're not friendly where you work?' asked someone. 'We're all in this together, after all.'

I shook my head. 'In "Intelligence"? I sometimes think there are English words they have never known the meaning of.'

'Like "Hello"?' asked Dr Dayne.

I nodded.

'Of course they don't know "Hello",' quipped someone else. 'It should be "G'day", shouldn't it?'

I blew raspberries, as they laughed at this quintessentially Australian joke.

After that I frequently exercised and breakfasted with them. Not every day, but most, and my muscles and arthritis improved to the point where I could walk upright without pain and was able to do my part when furniture or equipment needed moving around in our office. This meant I was almost normal physically, but I still had problems with Humans. Apart from when I was with the medical bunch who had seen all sorts, and were themselves a touch eccentric, I was still withdrawn.

One day, ducking across the camp in the rain, I bumped into a woman coming the other way, both of us hurrying and not watching where we were going. She looked vaguely familiar, but I couldn't place her. I shrugged it off, thinking maybe she had stayed at the hotel at some stage, and continued on my way, promptly forgetting all about it.

As I came into the canteen later that day to collect an evening meal before scampering away to my room, the woman stepped in front of me. I automatically stepped sideways trying to avoid whomever was blocking my way.

'Jack. It is you, isn't it, Jack?'

I looked at her and shook my head and tried to step around her again.

She put an arm on my shoulder and I froze. 'Jack. It's me, Patricia. Your wife.'

I had no wife. What was she talking about?

'Jack, we're both here.'

Who? Both whom?

'Your son, and me.'

'[That's not possible].' I knew she had to be mistaking me for someone else. 'I don't know who you think I am, but you've got the wrong [Human].'

Her face froze in a rictus of anger. 'Don't you play that game with me.' She raised her chin. 'You owe me four years' child support!'

I shook my head, '[No].' and broke free, moving towards the counter.

'Jack! They said you were crazy, but to deny your own flesh and blood, Jack?'

I frowned, puzzled at her. I was willing to accept "crazy". I knew I didn't always react in a Human manner, but "flesh and blood"? I shook my head. 'Happy to do a DNA test,' I said.

'Oh, you!' She stormed out of the canteen.

Feeling really confused, I continued to the counter.

'You should count yourself lucky you have a family,' said the person behind the counter. He sounded really hostile.

I shrugged. 'I have no idea who she is.' I could feel him continuing to glare as I made my selection from what little was left.

But she came in to work the next day with a child. She thrust the little one at me, saying, 'John, say "hello" to your father.'

I stood up, eyes wide, feeling the fury coursing through my veins. '[How dare you]?' I said. 'That … that … cruel, cruel trick to play on a child. [How could you do it? To your own child]?'

She recoiled, grabbing the child and pulling him away from me, where before she had thrust him at me. 'You owe us.'

'[I owe you nothing, Human]!' I advanced on her, my hands clenched. 'Nothing!'

'Whoa, Ale, stop.' My colleagues rushed to hold me back.

I let them. My anger evaporated as suddenly as it arrived, leaving me deflated and exhausted.

Our supervisor stepped forward, wanting to know what was going on, and this Human creature who called herself my wife thrust a piece of paper at him. He glanced at it and passed me a birth certificate for a "John Patrick Stevens", son of Patricia and Jack Stevens. It meant nothing to me. I gave it back with a shrug. I knew I wasn't Ale, but I was equally sure I wasn't Jack Stevens either.

We were a weird mob in Intelligence, and my supervisor confirmed it by turning to the boy and asking, 'How many times has she asked you to pretend in front of some poor schmuck that he's your father? And how many times has it succeeded?'

On one level it worked, because the kid stopped looking as though he'd been stabbed in the heart, and instead gaped at him.

But it was her turn to be furious. 'I'm not lying. That's four years' child support you owe me. I'll get it, you'll see. You're still my husband. I'm entitled to some of your pay.'

'I get paid?' I asked stupidly.

Someone snorted.

She glared and dragged the poor kid out.

My supervisor rolled his eyes and tugged his left earring, a habit he had when thinking deeply. 'Got any more surprises like that, Ale?'

'Hope not.'

'Yeah.' He shooed us all back to work.

Over breakfast the next morning, I asked Roger (Dr Dayne) if he could do a DNA test.

'Can do the test for you,' he said. 'Got no idea who I can get to analyse the results though. Why?'

I told him and the others present about my encounter with Patricia Stevens and her son.

'Shit out of luck with the child support, isn't she? When was the last time you actually earnt an income?' asked Bill.

I blew a raspberry and smiled. 'The day [the General's people] arrived. They took over the hotel on Day One.'

'That's three and a half years. Thought you said you were with them two and a half years.'

'I was under the [General]'s direct control for two and a half years. They put the Hotel under Drander's control the day they landed in Melbourne.'

'Wait, Drander is one of "them"?'

'Drander's People are ... are Prisoners of War, like us.'

'I've heard you say so much about her, I just assumed she was your partner.'

'She was ... is. We ran the hotel together. Kind of like a business partnership.'

'More than that, I would have said,' muttered Bill, but he let the subject drop.

I half dropped my eyelids, thinking about his remark. The [General] had seemed to think there was something more between us too.

A couple of days after that, my supervisor's manager came into the office and slammed a copy of the birth certificate on my desk. 'I have better things to do with my time than deal with people's domestics. Fix this.'

I wanted to say I had better things to do with my time too. It had nothing to do with me, so why did I have to fix it?

But that night, after eating, I tracked her down to the room she shared with two other women and their children. She came out into the corridor to talk with me.

Being in Intelligence, I had a private room, but I'd come to realise this was a luxury few people shared. Even Roger slept in a room with five other Doctors in the hospital—when, that is, any of them slept.

'We need to talk.'

'I knew you'd come to your senses sooner or later, Jack.' She threw her arms around me and tried to kiss me.

Her breasts pressed against my chest and certain parts of my body started to respond in a very physical way. It had been a long, long time since I'd had sex. But as I bent to return her proffered kiss, my nose encountered hers. And I felt ... revulsion.

Drander and I had never kissed. I'd spent most of my time actively avoiding all physical contact with her, but subconsciously my mind had expected to encounter a noseless face. And Patricia Stevens had a nose, which got in the way.

I held her at arms' length, feeling nauseated.

'I'm sorry, lady, but I really do not know who you are. The child cannot be mine, and even if it was, you won't get anything from me, because I don't have anything. Even the clothes I'm wearing were someone else's once.'

I hadn't asked Bill where they'd come from. I wasn't sure I wanted to know the answer.

'The hotel. What have you done to our hotel?'

'My hotel.' I corrected her automatically, and my heart contracted, as I remembered a similar argument I'd had with someone else. 'The Aliens have it.'

All the fight went out of her and she sagged against the wall. 'You really don't remember me?'

I shook my head.

'If your name isn't "Jack", what is it, then?'

'I don't remember that either. People call me "Ale".'

'So, I really could be your wife, and you wouldn't know?' she said with a hint of hope in her voice.

I looked at her coldly. 'If you are my wife, I want a divorce.' I could not conceive of being married to someone who would treat a child as she had treated her son the previous day.

Where Drander would have blinked at me, her eyes widened. At their widest they were still smaller than Drander's. I walked away.

Shortly after that we moved. I was issued a plastic bag, with a label that had my name on it, and told to pack my belongings. That was easy—my gym clothes and my change of clothes—all second hand. I quite literally owned nothing. Having done that, I helped dismantle our office and get it onto the trucks. Within eight hours, the whole camp had been dismantled and we moved about a five-hour drive away.

Then reassembled everything.

I tumbled into my newly assigned bed, exhausted. The whole operation, including moving the hospital and gym, had taken less than a day.

The next day I could hardly move for the pain. I sought out the physio and actually allowed her to massage me. She chided me as she tortured my aching body. 'You may be thirty-five years old chronologically, Mr Ale, but you have the physique of a man twice that age. Take better care of yourself.'

And here I'd been thinking I was improving.

I found Bill taking a smoko, as I tried to remember where my office had gone.

'Where are we?' I asked.

He shrugged. 'No idea any more. No idea where we came from either. Or the move before that. Or the one before that. I joined them in the Dandenongs but that was ages ago. It's not as though you or I have got anywhere else to be, after all.'

I looked away from him.

He looked sharply at me. 'Oh, no. Ale. You can't! He'll just grab you again.'

'I have to know if they're alright,' I whispered fiercely.

'We've all got family we left behind, or mislaid along the way.' He paused. 'All of us. You can't go back there till this is over.'

'If!'

'When. People like you are making a huge difference to this battle.'

He was right, of course, but I didn't want to hear it. 'I want to go home.' I whimpered. 'When this is over, Drander will be gone.'

'Then the hotel will be yours again.'

I shook my head. 'You don't understand. She risked her life for us. We harboured known fugitives in the hotel, right under their noses. We fed refugees with food bought with their money. I ...' I wasn't quite ready to tell anyone how she had helped to turn me into "the baby assassin".

'She betrayed her own people?'

'[No]! It's complicated, but we are not at war with Drander's people. Just [the General's people].'

'Um?'

'Drander's people are just as much victims as we are. Our war is with the ... the crocodile people.'

'I don't think they differentiate,' he said drily, nodding to the rest of the camp.

'I know.' Miserably I reached for one of his cigarettes.

He held them away from me. 'No way. I was willing to let you have one when I thought it would save your life, but I am not going to let you use them to commit slow suicide. Bad enough I smoke. Besides they're really hard to get hold of. Every time we move, I have to track down new suppliers for everything, including these.'

'Save my life?'

'Yeah. Don't you remember how you were that morning?'

I did.

And he was right.

I leant against the gumtree we were standing under, sheltering from the cold wind. Looked up at the sparse canopy above. It was just over halfway through winter and all the trees around us were in bloom. I pulled a gum flower down and sniffed its sharp fresh fragrance. Looked at the delicate stamens poking out, red with yellow tips. In that moment of time it was the most wondrous thing I'd ever seen.

Bill silently puffed downwind of me.

I looked up and caught him watching. 'I still want to go home.'

'Don't we all, mate?' He stubbed out his cigarette. 'C'mon. Lessee if I can find you a warmer jacket.'

The very next day they caught a [ship person] and brought it to the camp. I was asked to translate.

It was hurt.

'[What have they done to you]?' I cried, hurrying over to it.

It smiled. 'Heeeero.'

I stopped in front of it and bowed. 'I'm so sorry.'

It spat and I opened my mouth to receive it gladly, smiling, absurdly happy. Around me the soldiers and others gasped and some even gagged. I almost hugged it, so great was my gratitude, but it was hurt. I put my hand over one of the seeping wounds, gently.

'[Can't you heal this]?'

'[Can't reach].'

I held my hand up and it spat again. Carefully I spread the spit on the worst of its wounds. I ran out, and it spat again. I spread it carefully over one of its wings.

'[Do you ever see Drander]?' I asked, as I worked.

'[Yes].'

'[Can you get a message to her]?'

'[Yes].'

'[Tell her I'm alive. Ask about] Robin. [I need to know if he's okay].'

It was silent for a while as I continued to administer to it. The [Humans] around seemed frozen with shock.

'Robiiin. [He does not move. Has not moved in a long time].'

I cried out and leant against it. *My Robin, my beautiful trusting Robin. What had I done?* It put an arm around my shoulder.

'[Can you fix him]? Please. [I give up my place in your ship for him. Heal him].'

Our Glorious Leader asked, 'What's happening?'

We both ignored him.

'[Your egg]?'

'[Not from here],' I said touching my groin. '[From here].' I touched my heart.

'Aaah.'

Then it nodded. '[She will bring the egg to us].'

I bowed again. 'Thank you. Thank you.' A huge, huge weight lifted itself from my shoulders, and I turned to look at the assembled Humans. 'This is a [ship person],' I said. 'They are neutral. Your fight is not with them. Think of them as the Swiss in the Second World War.'

'The Swiss harboured fugitives,' said a soldier with a long band of stars on his epaulette. None of the soldiers had pristine uniforms, but this one looked better than most. I figured him to be a local General or some such.

'Yes,' I said, and let that sink in. '[The ship people] are off limits. Return this one,' I said directly to our leader.

'Or what?'

'Quite frankly, I wouldn't want to find out. Even "They" respect [the ship people]'s neutrality,' I said.

He stared at me. Like all Humans, his eyes were too small to be effective. He was nothing. But the person standing beside me, with a forearm leaning nonchalantly on my shoulder, had just given me back my family, and was going to fix my Robin. I tilted my head and stared back, eyelids half-lowered.

It was our Leader who backed down. 'Do as he says,' he said uncomfortably to the soldiers, and turned to me. 'Go with them to make sure it gets there safely.'

They protested, of course. He looked at me. Neither of us had moved. We made him really uncomfortable. He had the good sense to realise when he was beaten.

We were bundled, none too gently, into the back of a land rover, and driven off. I wondered why they didn't blindfold us, but then realised they thought, with the first layer of eyelid down, that it was blind. I didn't enlighten them. I knew it wouldn't give us away. But there was one message I did need to get back to the [General].

'[Tell the General I did not carry to term. It was stillborn]. I'm sorry.' I had spent long enough in the nursery to know the correct technical terms.

'[Did you eat the egg]?'

'[Is that what they do]?'

'[It repairs and prepares for the next egg].'

I shook my head. '[That is not our way. I dealt with it according to our way].'

It nodded.

'[Besides, I don't want to be prepared for any more of their 'eggs']!'

It blew raspberries. It was good not to be the odd one out as I joined in.

We let [the ship person] go on a hilltop in sight of the ship, but out of sight of the Alien camp just beyond. It flew off using its now healed wings.

On the way back, the soldiers let me know how they felt about having to return their prize. They were not as adept at it as the [General]'s staff had been.

I might have been able to ignore it, but Bill and the others took great exception to the bruises they left on my torso.

'What the hell is that?' our (as in the hospital's) canteen manager, Michelle, asked as I stripped off to get changed the next morning.

'What?' I asked, trying to look at my back.

'It's not just your back, Ale.' Bill was in front of me and staring too.

I looked where he was looking. There were a couple of dark purple bruises, one just above my heart, and another near a kidney. 'Oh that. It seems Soldiers are the same the galaxy over. I was just the nearest available victim.'

'*We* did that to you?'

I shrugged. 'Yeah. It's no big deal. There's no actual damage done.'

But Roger pushed forward and insisted on examining me. I rolled my eyes and shivered in my underwear and did everything he asked me to, while a bunch of the others, including Bill watched anxiously.

At length he let me get dressed, a puzzled frown on his face. 'I want to do X-rays again.'

'I'm okay. I feel fine.'

'That's just it. When did you last feel fine? You don't complain or anything, but I'd be a lousy doctor if I didn't know you were in pain all the time. Besides we can normally hear your joints cricking when you move.'

A murmur of "hear hear", and other words of confirmation issued from the onlookers.

He had a point. I licked my lips and noticed, as my tongue slid past my teeth, that they no longer hurt as much either. 'Okay.'

'Good. I'll let you know when it is booked.'

They didn't complain either, but that alone told me how busy they were.

Later the same day, our Leader sent for me. He wanted to "chat". He wasn't happy about losing a potential source of information like the [ship person]. I thought about the sort of information a [ship person] might have been willing to provide, which they (the Humans) wouldn't already know, and said, 'Have you thought of asking me?'

'What?'

'I did spend some time with the [General]. It was his child I was carrying.'

'What?'

And as that sunk in, he asked, 'Why didn't you say?'

'No-one asked.'

'What do you mean?'

To everyone, even my own department, I was just that crazy demented person who was so badly damaged that he thought he was an Alien. Only my friends in the hospital saw through the involuntary mannerisms to the person beneath, and they were more concerned with my wellbeing than my potential as a source of knowledge.

'Who debriefed you?'

'What?'

'All released prisoners get debriefed. Who debriefed you?'

I shook my head. '[Nobody.] Must've slipped through the net when you sent me straight to Intelligence to decipher those shopping lists.'

Not that it would have helped at that time. When I first arrived, I was barely speaking English. I would have had trouble understanding what they wanted anyway.

'Right. Of course.' He smiled ruefully. 'Your own department do the debriefings, but ...'

'I was already one of them by then.'

He nodded. 'Come on.'

And back to my department we went, where I was sat down at my desk and my colleagues were "invited" to chat with me about my experiences.

I explained about the social structure of the three different groups.

Then I gave them information on the [General].

Why not? Now that the guilt at having lost his baby had been assuaged, I no longer felt I owed him anything. And I had a lot to give. I had spent almost a year in his war room as a captive, and even after I'd left it he'd come to see me regularly, pouring out his innermost thoughts and concerns on what he had assumed was a disinterested party.

I might not remember my name, but I remembered everything I had seen or heard in that war room and every word he'd ever said to me. At the time his visits had been the only thing I had to live for. I did bow my head and shed a tear as I realised just how much of a betrayal this was, but, I knew, had the roles been reversed he would not have hesitated, so I ploughed on.

It took us three days, after which I was so exhausted, I slept around the clock.

I woke to discover I had a bodyguard.

It was too late for breakfast at the general cafeteria, so I went to the hospital canteen where Michelle supplied meals for patients and staff twenty-four hours a day.

'Technically I shouldn't be serving you,' she said as she made me a milkshake and a sandwich.

'I know. I'm hungry.' I was ravenous—the hungriest I had been for some time.

She smiled. 'That's what they all say. Rog,' (Dr Dayne) 'said to tell you the X-ray is booked for seventeen hundred hours.'

'What? He asked you to pass the message on? Why can't he?'

'We haven't been able to get near you for four days. It was originally scheduled for yesterday, but they said you were not to be disturbed.'

'They? Who they?'

'Security. What have you been up to?' She nodded to my bodyguard, who was pretending to be just leaning against a random wall.

I shook my head. 'Nothing.'

'First they beat you up—'

I'd forgotten about that.

'Then they put a security detail on you.' She heaved a sigh. 'It ain't "nothing". I'm willing to accept that it's hush hush given where you work, but "nothing"? No. No, I can't believe that.'

If I'd had two eyelids, I would have dropped them halfway.

She said, 'And now you've gone all Alien inscrutable on me—'

'I've what?' I blinked at her.

She rolled her eyes. 'Just eat, Ale lad. And go and see Roger at seventeen hundred hours. Okay?'

Back at work, I was told to go see the psychologist.

'When?'

'As soon as you wake up.'

Wondering what was so important it couldn't wait for a proper appointment, I went back across camp with my poor bodyguard trailing after me. The psychologist on duty made room for me by ignoring her next patient and letting me straight in, sourly telling me I had become priority number one.

'Why?'

She didn't answer that. But she did ask me how I was doing at adjusting to Human society again.

'Mostly I avoid [Humans].'

'It has been so noted,' she said. 'Do you remember anything from before the Aliens arrived? Your name?'

'[No].'

'Are you Human?'

I blinked at her and remembered to nod.

'I have the task of trying to make you remember your humanity.' She made it sound like an impossibility.

Maybe it was.

She took me back to my childhood days, but even that was fraught with minefields.

I remembered school days of unrelenting stress and pressure. Of constantly being compared to someone, and being found wanting. I remembered my parents' shame when I was kicked out of law school, their confusion as they realised I really didn't care, and their sorrow when I dumped the surname "McMurphy" and went bush. I couldn't remember why I had done this to them, just that I had. Nor could I remember the name I had replaced McMurphy with.

I finished my session with her, feeling I was a failure at life, both Human and Alien.

Back at work again, our Leader dropped in. 'It called you "Hero",' he reminded me.

I shrugged. 'Maybe that's my name in their language, or maybe it's just a random English word. They don't really speak our language.'

'Oh. You sure that's it?'

I didn't actually answer him. He just assumed I assented and left us. I prepared to get back to work, but our supervisor pulled the folder on my desk out of reach and handed it to someone else.

'Ale,' he said quietly, 'you can't work here if we cannot trust you. And we cannot trust you if you continue to deliberately keep secrets from us.'

'You never asked about the [General] before,' I said.

He folded his arms and shook his head. His earrings today were fake pearls on a short chain, el cheapo costume jewellery, but they momentarily distracted me as they waved about. Someone close to me had once had a pair like it but it was a guilty secret between us, though I couldn't remember who.

My supervisor misinterpreted my frown and went over to a filing cabinet. He placed a piece of paper on my desk in front of me. The "wanted" notice with a picture of me in Drander's hoodie.

'This was in your pocket. This was the only thing in your pockets.'

I touched the picture. That hoodie had been so silky soft and light, yet so warm. And the colouring had been just right for nocturnal strikes, blending perfectly into the background at night. It really did seem like a lifetime ago. I had been "Ale" in that life too. And for the first time I wondered what Drander had been doing with such an object in her possession.

Someone started reading the notice over my shoulder, at first sounding out the Alien words, then after each phrase, slowly translating it.

They got to 'Worm Assassin' and I corrected them. 'Grub. Their babies look more like Witchetty Grubs, than worms.'

You could have heard a pin drop in the office.

My supervisor picked the picture back up and looked at it more closely. 'Did the [General] know?' he asked.

I nodded and looked up at him.

'Was'—he gestured to indicate a pregnant state—'a punishment?'

I shook my head. 'Not the first one. Not my punishment anyway. The first one was a punishment for Drander. I killed it—aborted it. The rest were a punishment for that, not ...' I gestured to the piece of paper. I looked back down at my hands on the desk. They no longer looked like talons, but they were still much bonier than I'd been used to.

'He tagged them. He tagged my staff—all of them, even the children,' I whispered. 'He knows exactly where they are all the time. If Drander or I step out of line, they get punished. That's the way it works. When Drander displeased him, I got punished. When I displeased him, they got punished. And they can't run away.' I felt the tears welling up and let them come.

My supervisor frowned. 'Did he punish them when we freed you?'

I shook my head. 'I don't know. [The ship person] didn't say.'

'Why not?'

'They are neutral. They don't get involved.'

'But they call you "Hero".'

I shrugged.

'Is this tagging of Humans common?'

I shook my head. 'All Drander's people are tagged, but it was unheard of till then to do it to Humans.'

'How could we tell?'

I pinched the skin on my neck just above the collar bone and below the pulse point. 'Little round piece of firmware. Try not to nick the jugular when removing it.'

'I'll pass this information on to the medical staff who do the initial processing.'

'They already know. Told them weeks ago.'

'Your friends?'

I nodded.

He sighed and nodded. 'I've got a new assignment for you.'

He beckoned to Brett, the oldest person on our team. 'Brett is an anthropologist. He was most recently doing a government study with Sydney's homeless, and then the refugees. I want you to work with Brett, and see if, between you, you can come up with a plausible social structure for the three groups of Aliens. And when you've done that, I want you to grab a dictionary and see if you can match each word to an Alien word—usage and spelling. Alright?'

'Big job.'

He nodded. 'You're the best person for it.'

'Sir?'

He waited.

'Why do I have a bodyguard?'

'I hear you've already been attacked once.'

I shrugged. 'Just soldiers being soldiers.'

'Yeah, well, you've just become the most valuable person in camp, and I don't want them trying anything else on you.'

Wondering how fortunes could change so radically, I made space for Brett beside me.

At the appointed time I went across to the hospital and let the radiologist take the X-rays of my major joints, my backbone, and my teeth. They were processed while I had tea over there, nodding "hello" to a very busy Michelle.

Then Roger sought me out and took me back to his office to show me the miracle which had been transpiring. My teeth were completely healed—I could have told him that—and my bones had started to lay calcium down, while the ossification in my joints had almost disappeared.

'You're still not cured,' he said. 'You've still got the bones of a fifty-year-old, but you are in much better shape than you were a month ago. Given care and regular exercise, there is no reason why you shouldn't now live to a ripe old age. And,' he added pointing to the X-ray of my mouth, 'you glow.'

I looked, and he was right. The gum line did indeed glow faintly. Like Drander's tears.

'Want to tell me what's going on? Should I be isolating you?'

'Bit late for that, isn't it?' I touched my scar and told him how [the ship people]'s spit had healing properties which seemed to work on us as well.

'Pity we can't bottle it,' he said with a sigh.

'They are off-limits. Even the crocodile people respect that.'

'[The General's people]?' he asked doing a passable rendition of the word.

'[Yes].'

On the second Saturday after the move, we had a camp tradition—a dance. Only on that Saturday, the second after a move, did they feel safe enough to down tools and enjoy themselves like this. (On the first they were still ironing out resettlement issues.)

Like everyone else, despite the crowds of [Humans], I went along. Mindful of Roger's injunction that I was still older than my body should be, I was careful. I had a few dances with various members of my gym group, drank a couple of drinks whilst yelling across the noise at one of my colleagues from Intelligence, and then one with Bill. Then I did a circuit of the room just watching and actually enjoying myself for the first time that I could remember in a long time, despite the crowds. I passed a booth in which three children were sitting hunched over the remains of a plate of Nachos. One of them looked like that woman's child, John.

'Hi,' I said.

He looked up miserably.

'Don't want to be here?' I asked.

He nodded.

'Our mother says we have to sit here and not get in anyone's way,' said one of the other children.

'Why aren't you back in your room?'

'No-one to babysit us,' said the other unknown.

'Where's Patricia?' I asked John.

He shrugged.

I went in search of her. Found her dancing with a soldier with stripes on his uniform. I could appreciate the effort she'd made to be attractive without feeling the least bit affected.

I told her, 'I'm putting John and his friends to bed.'

Her eyes widened in surprise, but she acquiesced rapidly enough.

So I went back and told them I had Patricia's permission. They came gladly, just stopping to grab the other child they shared a room with, before we headed out. On the way, we bumped into Michelle who goggled at the sight of me with four children in tow. I invited her to join us which she readily agreed to.

There was a small fridge in the room with a couple of litres of milk in it, so I gave them each a drink, and then made them clean their teeth.

'You're not our father, we don't have to do what you tell us,' the eldest loftily informed me.

'Your father ain't here, I am,' I replied forcefully, pointing down the hall to the shared bathroom.

If I could stare down the leader of our country's resistance forces, I could certainly manage one nine or ten-year-old boy. He picked up his toiletry bag and resentfully led the way.

John trailed behind. 'Aren't you my father?' he asked in a forlorn voice.

'I'm sorry,' I told him, brushing a lock of hair off his forehead. 'I can't be.'

'Who is my father then?'

'I have no idea. Ask your Mother.'

'She says you are.'

'I'm sorry. She's wrong. I can't be anyone's Dad.'

'You don't know your name, but you're sure you're not a father,' said Michelle, as he disappeared into the bathroom with the others.

'[Yes].' But I couldn't remember or understand why I knew that.

Back in the room, I tucked the children into their beds. I amused them by singing a lullaby Drander had taught us trying to get Justine to sleep. They laughed at the funny sounds of the Alien language and tried to imitate them. When the hilarity had died down, I told them the story of the ugly duckling. Then I turned the lights out, and Michelle and I sat talking softly on one of the adults' beds until they were asleep. She volunteered to stay with them until one of the mothers showed up.

So I went back to the dance in time to roll a drunken Bill, who had reached the maudlin stage, to the dormitory he shared in the hospital. As I stripped him and put him to bed, he said, 'You remind me of Josh. You are sooo like him.'

Josh and I are nothing alike. I wondered who Josh was that I actually cared whether I was like him or not.

And back to the dance, this time to assist in handling the more belligerent drunks. Between my publican know how and my bodyguard's brawn—he wasn't about to let me do it on my own, so was forced to assist—we manhandled quite a few to what passed as a brig in the informal atmosphere of the camp, there to sleep off the drink.

Again, back to the dance in time for the slow dances. Michelle rejoined us, and we danced those last few dances together. And, joy of joys, she consented to come back to my room afterwards.

And if my first effort, even with a condom on, was far too eager to satisfy either of us, the second made up for it, if her contented sigh as she snuggled down to sleep beside me was anything to go by. She didn't even seem to mind that I felt uncomfortable with mouth kissing, both of us finding plenty of other places for that activity.

In the morning she went off to gym at the usual time. I figured I'd done enough exercise in the last twenty-four hours and declined the invitation to join her, preferring to enjoy the post coital haziness. She gave me a long lingering hug and thanked me for a wonderful evening. I told her the pleasure was all mine, and we both meant it. For the first time I could remember I was relaxed and happy.

Nothing would come of it, of course. This was strictly a case of "what happens in camp stays in camp". She had mislaid a husband somewhere between Sydney and the resistance fighters' camp and was eager to get back after the fighting to try to find him. And me? I didn't even know my own name, let alone my marital status. For all I knew, Patricia could really be telling the truth. My gut told me otherwise though.

On Monday I had another session with the psychologist. She asked me to remember my most recent happy memory before coming to camp. I thought about it. It was a couple of years old, the memory of the [General]'s baby swimming free and happy in the tub before either of us realised what was in store for it. This startled her.

'Further back,' she commanded.

Further back? Drander coming to visit me, getting the blood singing through my veins, and giving me the goss on the hotel in the two sentences she was allowed.

'Further.'

Something was making her uneasy.

There was the day I woke up after an afternoon nap pinned down by the combined weights of Karen, Justine, and Robin, with Drander smiling tenderly down on us. She was okay with this memory until I mentioned that last detail.

'Further.'

One of those rare moments of relaxation when one day was over and preparation for the next was still in the planning stages, and the kitchen staff sitting down sharing a drink and just talking.

'Go on.'

The women joining us and Drander automatically sitting beside me and taking a sip of my drink. I said something which made her blow raspberries so violently she choked, and I'd had to rescue both her and the glass.

The psychologist sighed. 'Further.'

My gratitude when the ship person agreed to heal Karen's cut after the stones were thrown at them? No, that was an unacceptable memory too. It had a [ship person] in it. I was working out the pattern now.

So, a purely Human memory. The perfect day. I skipped over the start of the day when I was offered sanctuary by [the ship people] and spoke of the hour spent in Justine and Robin's company. Then I told her about enrolling the older children in school, and the pretty picture the three of them made propping each other up, dozing, whilst waiting for the principal. I skipped the intermediate activity when Justine and Robin and I had arrived home, and Jenny had scolded Robin and me for making a mess with the chocolate, while Drander, blowing soft raspberries, had fetched a cloth and cleaned them both up.

Happy with the session, she finally let me go.

But I was really confused. How was it that so many of my happy memories included my so-called "Master"? And when was the last time she had, in fact, acted like a "Master"? So many memories were of her reaching out to comfort me. And while I was still mobile, I had persistently shrugged her off. And now I was finding, despite Michelle, and Bill, and Rog and the others, I actually missed her.

I found Bill in the medical stores area.

'You look like Josh whenever he went to see his dad. Wondering if you're destined for Hell in the afterlife because your best friend isn't the same as everyone else's,' he said.

'Yeah, well. I've just been with the psychologist.'

'Errk.'

'Do you think I'm wrong to love a ... one of Drander's kind?'

'Do you?' he asked straight back to me.

I thought of her many kindnesses, to me, to the children. Of her bickering with her batchling. A tear slid down my cheek, 'Do you think any the worse of me because of what I love?' I asked him

'Do you think any the worse of me because of what I love?' he asked in response.

I looked at him.

'Oh, come on. You can't say you haven't realised I'm gay.'

'Oh, that. My brother ...' I started to say my brother was gay too, but did I actually have a brother? Had I ever had a brother?

'Your brother's name wouldn't happen to be Josh, would it?' Bill smiled gently at my confusion. 'You are getting more and more like him now that you're putting the weight back on.'

I shook my head. I didn't know my own name, so how was I expected to remember someone whom I-wasn't-sure-existed's name.

'He had a twin. John.'

John McMurphy. It sounded familiar. Or was I just thinking that, because Patricia called her son John? Besides, she said my name was Jack.

I shook my head and shrugged apologetically at him. 'I don't know. I just don't know.'

'Ah well, never mind. It'll come to you when you're ready.'

'Whatcha doing?'

'Hunting up drips. They should be in the fridge, but they're not. We've got incoming. Some of them are apparently in a similar state to you when you came to us. I hope they haven't gone off, they're so hard to get hold of.'

He meant the drips, not the incoming. Well, I was sure if I could find a 1967 Merlot or a 1982 Federation Port on request, I could find a large blue cooler, so I helped him in the search. We found four, transferred them to the fridge, and I left him taking three drips across to triage, while I wandered back to my dictionary work.

A few days after that, we encountered each other in the middle of the quadrangle in the early hours of the morning. I had managed to lose my bodyguard and had just come back from escorting Michelle back to the hospital. I didn't ask whose room he was coming back from, or what he was doing there. Even if Josh was my brother, Camp Liaisons were none of anyone's business except the participants.

He'd been absent from gym the last couple of mornings, so I stopped to say "hello". I started to ask him about the three people who'd been brought in "like me", when I heard the sound of alien ships above.

'[Run]!' I yelled, and, grabbing his hand, ran for the nearest perimeter.

'What?' he gasped, but he followed anyway.

'Incoming!' I shrieked, as we passed the guards.

I didn't stay to see what they did. In the dark, Bill and I stumbled on until we came up against an overhang he had often taken shelter under while he smoked.

There we turned and looked back at the camp, just as the first incendiaries streaked from the sky. Within seconds the camp was ablaze and pandemonium broke loose. In the fiery light we could see people fleeing our direction, but then came the "pops" I'd heard years before and they fell one by one. Bill cried out and would have run back had I not thrown myself on him.

'There'll be people hurt!' he cried, trying to squirm out from under me.

'Danger!' I yelled at him, hanging on. 'Wait till it's safe.'

And I prayed he remembered the Dr ABCD mantra which dictated that all medical people check for danger to themselves before offering aid to anyone else.

He squirmed under me some more but then a bomb landed near enough to us to kick dirt and branches in my face, and he suddenly became still. So still, I thought he'd been hit.

Frightened, I moved back to look more closely at him. He took the opportunity to squirm onto his belly, and lying flat, looked back at the camp. I was so relieved I hugged him. Tears streaming down his face, he hugged back.

'How did you know?' he whispered.

'I heard them.'

'I heard nothing.'

'We used to listen for them, Drander and I. We had four hours after they landed until they descended on the hotel. It gave us time to be prepared.'

He looked oddly at me for a second, opened his mouth to say something, but then another bomb landed in our direction and lit up the few people who had made it this far. In silent horror we watched them being shot from above, crumbling mere feet from our sheltered position.

After that we didn't dare move for hours. Watching the flames, listening to the "pops", and eyeing the dead in front of us.

'Welcome to Hell,' I whispered when the "pops" finally ceased.

'I'm going back,' he whispered in return. 'There may be someone we can save.'

I didn't think it was likely, but it was worth a try, so we picked our way back to the camp by the light of the dying fires, keeping to the dark as much as we could.

The camp was a flattened mess. No structure was left standing. Bill sank down on his knees in front of the mound that used to be the hospital and covered his face. I left him there and wandered over to what remained of the living quarters. In an absurd way, even though I knew it wasn't the case, I felt this was retribution for all those deaths I'd caused all those years ago. It just felt inevitable. Unlike Bill, I didn't seem to have any feelings to express. I wandered among the dead, muttering Latin prayers, remembered from my childhood, for their souls, comforted by the familiar meaningless sounds. I hadn't been to church since I left school, but somehow it seemed the right thing to do.

Somebody whimpered.

'Bill,' I called, 'over here!' and started in on the mound nearest the sound.

It seemed at first that all we were doing was uncovering more dead, and pieces of bodies. And nurse though he was, Bill had to stop to vomit when I heaved someone's torso out of the way. That caused me to stop and think about what I was moving. I couldn't feel the same way he did. For weeks in a past life I had stepped over and between the corpses in the park. I had done my crying and gotten over my squeamishness years ago. The 'Dead' were just that. Dead. And right now, they were an obstacle to the living.

'Where are you?' I called softly.

A moan.

Bill remembered why we were here, and helped me move another body, suddenly determined and focused.

More rubble, then another body. I gasped and doubled over in pain myself this time. 'Patricia,' I whispered, and suddenly the tears were coming. 'John! John, are you there?'

Another moan, and we could see his arm moving. Patricia's body had protected the boy's body from the worst of the explosion. Bill carefully lifted a bit of building resting on top of him. I wanted him to go so much faster, but even I knew the danger of sudden removal of foreign objects from a wound.

Clear.

John turned to look at us, crying with pain at the sudden movement. There was darkness over the right side of his face. Blood? How bad was the damage?

Bill knelt beside him feeling up and down his small body and calmly asking questions.

John's vocabulary seemed to be restricted to whimpers, but he *was* responding.

Eventually Bill took a risk and picked him up, bringing him over to me.

'Oh, John.' I hugged him close. 'Thank God, you're alive.'

'Mr Ale?'

'Yes.'

'Where?' he asked. 'What?'

'Later,' I told him. 'Let's just get out of here.'

'Yeah,' agreed Bill, 'I can't see anyone else surviving this.'

We headed back the way we'd come, and just kept walking until daybreak, and when we were exhausted, lying down and sleeping huddled together for warmth on the ground where we stopped.

It was John's whimpering which woke us several hours later. Bill examined his face with a grim look.

'Well?' I asked.

'Too soon to tell. Need to get it clean.'

I licked my lips. 'I'm your friend, not your patient,' I said.

He had the grace to flush at the implied criticism. 'Sorry. I ... I really don't want to say, Ale. I'm sorry.'

'That bad, huh?'

He grimaced and picked up the little boy. 'Let's find a stream.'

We didn't find a stream; we got found by an Alien patrol instead. They herded us into a truck with other Human survivors and drove us to a nearby town where we were locked into the town hall.

No water, no facilities, and with every truckload the hall got more and more crowded. It wasn't just camp survivors being picked up. The local townspeople and the region's farmers were also being crammed in with us.

John started shivering and moaning.

Someone asked us to keep him quiet, and got blasted by his neighbour for insensitivity.

Shortly after that a bottle with a small amount of water made its way to us. I couldn't see where it had come from, so I just thanked the air. Bill ripped off the pocket of his shirt and wet it and the wound, but there wasn't a lot he could do with so little, and it was obviously hurting John to try, so he desisted. Instead we poured the water a sip at a time down his throat. He coughed and spluttered, but most of it got swallowed.

The day wore on, and night came with no relief. Somehow, we slept. John's fever got worse.

Daybreak came. Another day.

It was late afternoon by Bill's watch when we were ordered to stand and bunched into the centre of the room.

Then the most senior of the soldiers called out '[Kneel].'

'Down!' I yelled.

Bill and I both hit the floor on our knees. And then we clung to each other with John between us as the soldiers started mowing down anyone above waist height.

'[You two, come]!' the soldier ordered when it was over.

When I stared at him, still in shock, he raised his gun. '[I know you understand. Move].'

I stood and picked up John. Bill stood with me.

'[Follow].'

I felt the blood drain from my face. Why us? Had I been recognised?

'[Come].'

Trembling, I followed. Bill took his cue from me and came too.

We were loaded into a helicopter-like contraption and flown to a larger town. It was about the size of Bendigo, but it had been so long since I'd been down that way, I couldn't be sure where we were. They marched us into a posh hotel. Much better quality than my little place. Then into the lift and up to the top floor. What the hell was going on? Finally, we were shown to a room with a single bed and an en-suite and locked in.

'What?' whispered Bill when we were alone.

'I have no idea,' I told him, 'but we have running water. For now.'

'Right. Strip him. Let's get him under water.'

The shower recess had a shallow lip, so Bill placed the naked John in and turned on the water. I thought he'd use cold water to get his temperature down but the water that splashed down was lukewarm, and Bill just let it run over him and away. While he was doing that, I had a long drink of water using the only glass I could find, stripped off and washed our clothes. Then Bill and I swapped places. The caked blood was starting to dissolve from around John's wound, and we got a good look at the huge gash running down the right side of his face and through his eye. It was badly infected, and only a miracle was going to save that eye. If he lived. Even under water, he was still boiling to touch, and the wound just wasn't clearing.

John roused enough to realise he wasn't in Kansas any longer and cried and struggled against us. I kept telling him who I was and calling his name, and Bill just kept soothing him. I don't know if either of us were effective, but eventually he calmed down enough for us to give him some water, but then he slipped into unconsciousness and away from us again. Bill pulled him out of the shower, and I started drying him whilst Bill tried to devise a bandage from the bits and pieces of material we had in the room. He had the brilliant idea of using the pillow slip and stood up to go back into the bedroom.

'Um, A ... Ale? Ale?'

I looked up from John to see what was upsetting Bill so much.

The [General] was lounging just inside the bathroom door, looking amused.

I laid John down gently and prostrated myself. '[I'm sorry, Sir. I didn't hear you come in].'

'[I gather. Your hatchling]?'

'[His other parent says so].'

'[Give].' He held out one of his great hands.

I couldn't see anything else I could do, so I picked up John and reluctantly handed him over. Bill and I watched anxiously while the [General] examined the wound. He spat and John gasped and opened his other eye, staring in terror at the apparition in front of him. He started trembling, as well he might. The [General] frowned and shook his head.

He handed him back down to me. '[His other parent is wrong. You are compatible. He is not. He is not your hatchling. I cannot help him].' Was there regret in that deep voice? Then he focused on Bill. '[I ordered your return. I wasn't expecting you to arrive with company].'

'[I gathered].' I indicated the single towel and bed.

He twitched his ears and waited.

I sighed. '[He is my batchling's mate].' I didn't know if this was true or not, and whether I might be making Bill a hostage to my good behaviour, but it was the only explanation I could think of which the [General] might accept.

'[Your batchling]?'

I shrugged. '[We don't know where he is. Lots of people have gone missing. Him amongst them].'

'[I thought your kind are born as <something>, not in batches].'

'[Some of us are born in small batches of two or three. Sometimes more. My batch had two].'

I could see he was confused but he didn't let it bother him. '[You are looking much better than when I saw you last],' he said.

I looked at my toes. 'I'm sorry. [I lost the baby].'

'[You did better than most Humans. We have had to abandon that experiment].' He started to leave. '[I will send someone to help the hatchling].'

'[General]?'

He looked over his shoulder back at me. I had to do it. I couldn't not. 'I gave information about you to them.' I said it in English for Bill's benefit, knowing the [General] understood. Then I waited for his retaliation.

'[I did wonder at the sudden accuracy of their information],' he said and went out the door. We heard the lock click.

I slid to the floor, still holding John to me, and closed my eyes. I was hungry, I was tired, I was cold, I was holding a child who might not survive the night, and I was once again the [General]'s prisoner. And I didn't seem to be any closer to home and Drander. I started to cry.

Bill took John away and draped a blanket over me. He tiptoed around making a bandage for John's head, and then put him to bed, before coming and sitting beside me.

'I'm sorry,' I murmured into his shoulder.

He shrugged. 'Don't think either of us is exactly happy. I'd love a smoke.'

'Not gonna stop you,' I said.

He shook his head. 'I didn't have any on me.' He sounded slightly accusatory.

I snorted. 'What? You think I should have let you go back and get them before we ran for our lives?'

'No. Course not.' He grinned sheepishly.

'Daft head,' I said, punching him in the arm.

'Yeah,' he agreed. 'What will happen to us?'

'I told them you were my twin's partner.'

'They're okay with the gender thing?'

'I don't think they're even aware we have two genders.'

'But Drander is female, isn't she?'

'I have no idea. I call her a "her", and she asked the others to do the same, but I really don't know. And I call the [General] a "him", but he's the one who laid an egg in my stomach.'

And then I thought about those two hundred corpses that were put on display in the park and realised I had no idea which parent was which.

'I don't think gender has any relevance with them.'

'I wish,' he said bitterly. 'But that doesn't answer my question. What will happen to us?'

I shook my head. 'I don't know. He likes having me around. Someone to talk to. He said he specifically asked to have me back.'

'Like an exotic pet?'

I nodded, feeling the bile rise in my throat, as I realised that was quite probably what I was to the [General]. Was that how Drander felt about us? How could she feel that way about me? I couldn't believe it, she cared too much how we felt about her.

'Could be worse,' Bill said.

'How?'

'We're still alive.'

'That's supposed to be good? Sometimes it is the dead who are the lucky ones.' I went into the bathroom and cleaned myself up. My clothes were still damp, but I felt more comfortable with them back on.

Someone had delivered a tray with two plates of food while I was washing. It was purple stuff with a fungus sauce and mashed orange turnip stuff. Not my favourite meal but it was food, and we hadn't eaten in days. I sat down and started eating.

Bill looked at me aghast. 'That's edible?'

'Edible, yes. Palatable, no. Come and eat. Who knows when we'll be fed again.'

'I think I'd rather die.'

'He won't let you. Would you rather it this way or force-fed down a tube?' I couldn't bring myself to let him know I knew this first hand. He'd probably guess anyway, but I didn't want to talk about it. 'They're somewhat bigger and stronger than we are. If they want something, they tend to get it.'

Bill got the hint. He took his plate and dipped a cautious finger in the sauce.

'Don't waste it. You'll need it with the [purple stuff].'

'The ...?'

I picked up a piece and waved it at him. He turned a green colour and bolted for the bathroom. I could remember feeling like that once. I took a spoon over to John and tried to get some of the mash into his mouth. I was just in time to catch the resultant reaction on the tray.

'Neat idea, but he's not well enough. Wait here.' Bill disappeared back into the bathroom with the befouled tray.

I wondered idly where I was supposed to go.

When he came back out, dressed, he had the glass half full of water. He spooned some of the mash into it, and the sauce for good measure, and stirred it.

'Hold him.'

I got behind John and held him upright on my lap. Bill carefully spooned some of the mixture into his mouth. Then held his head up, keeping the mouth closed until John swallowed. That stayed down, so he risked another spoonful. On the third spoon John's stomach rebelled.

'Will he live?'

'If we can keep getting this stuff into him, then, yes, I think he might.' Bill actually sounded hopeful.

I held the boy's burning hot body to my own and had to trust Bill's professional judgement. We stayed that way about an hour, until a team of what we assumed were doctors came in and fussed over John. They replaced our makeshift bandage with a real one and smoothed some sort of cream over the wound. John cried out in pain as they did it, and I was ordered to keep him still and quiet. I held him tight until they left, taking the old bandage with them.

Bill gave him some more of the diluted mash. This time he managed to give John a fifth spoonful before the boy showed signs of regurgitation. He went into the bathroom again, and came out carrying a wet rag. It looked like he'd ripped our towel in two and wet one half of it. This he placed over John's hot body. At first John shuddered at the touch of the coldness, but his body quickly heated it up. After that Bill turned the lights out and curled up on the bottom of the bed and was asleep in seconds. I sat in the dark listening to his breathing and the whimpers of the little boy in my lap and wished I could be so carefree.

Exactly forty-five minutes later, Bill woke up and did it all again. 'Get some sleep,' he said to me as he once again curled up.

I did doze, because forty-five minutes later he woke me to repeat the exercise. And again, and again, over and over, all through the night. We ran out of mash in the early hours, so Bill just spooned water into John.

As the sky started turning grey, John roused enough to actually drink directly from the glass with our help, before settling down to sleep beside me.

I heard Bill sigh and looked up to see an exhausted but happy smile on his face.

'Danger over.' He high-fived me, tears in his eyes.

I couldn't help but admire his professionalism. All night at precise intervals he had woken up to administer to his patient, and not once had he let either of us know how frightened he'd been at what he would find. Not until now, when he knew he wouldn't find it.

I held my hand out to him and pulled him close enough to let him cry on my shoulder. 'I'm sorry. I'm supposed to be detached ...'

'But you're cold, you're hungry, you're exhausted, and you're terrified. I think anyone's allowed a little reaction in those circumstances, don't you?'

He smiled tremulously, 'I wouldn't say "terrified",' he murmured to the ground.

'Yeah? What would you say? Over the moon at the way things are going?'

He sighed and set about cleaning up. He didn't bother replacing the wet towel, and when he came back into the room, he grabbed our spare blanket and stretched out on the floor. Since everyone else was doing it, I lay down too, but sleep was still a long way off.

At some point in the morning, the doctor group came back and replaced John's bandage. They pulled out a needle to inject him, but Bill intervened.

'What is it?'

They replied with some word I'd never heard before. When it was clear neither of us understood, they tried again. '[To reduce <something>, help him fight <something else>].'

'I think it's antibiotics,' I told him.

'How do we know it's safe for him?'

I asked.

'[Made for him. We got his <something> last night. Created from that].' One of the doctors indicated the bandage on John's head.

My mouth gaped open. I didn't know they could do that. 'It's safe. It's made from his own DNA,' I told Bill.

'What?'

'I didn't know either. [Go ahead],' I said to them.

They nodded and injected him. He woke up enough to glare at them, before falling asleep again. This was the most alive we'd seen him since the attack, and Bill and I silently gave each other the thumbs up.

But exhaustion finally caught up with us both, and we just alternated between dozing and waiting. No-one brought us breakfast or lunch, so we just had the water. Bill refilled our bottle and tucked it into his shirt, just in case. John woke up around lunch time feeling a lot better physically but broke into tears when we couldn't produce his mother.

Again, I just held him.

When that eased off, I sang him Drander's lullaby. At least it was meant to be a lullaby, but it brought a smile to his face for a second. We tried playing "I Spy'" with him for a bit, but he was still a bit young for school and wasn't really well enough for mind games.

'Shall we just add boredom to the litany, and accept it as our lot in life?' I asked.

Bill sighed and paced. With John leaning against me, I didn't really have that option.

'If I knew what was going to happen in the next hour, I'd know whether it was worthwhile exercising or not,' Bill said.

Of course! Bill did gym every morning. I was the one who considered a night of horizontal gymnastics a sufficient excuse not to bother. Well, it beat sitting around doing nothing. I stood up and said, 'Okay.'

'Yeah? Okay.'

He then spent the next hour devising ways to keep our bodies in shape, while John lay on his belly on the bed and appeared to forget his misery, enough to grin at the spectacle we were making of ourselves anyway.

After a shower, we were back to just sitting again. I pushed our bed up to the only window, so we could at least look out while doing it. Not that there was a lot to see. We overlooked the car park at the back, and it was deserted. Occasionally one of Drander's people scurried around on some errand, one or two of the [General]'s people strode purposefully off somewhere. No Humans.

Bill climbed onto the bed and started examining the window for ways to open it and escape.

'Don't.'

'Why not?' said Bill, as he continued to prod at the window.

'He'll punish Drander.'

'You don't know that. You don't even know if they are still alive.'

'They were a couple of weeks ago.'

'What?' He sat down with a thump. 'How do you know?'

'That [ship person] spoke with one of them.'

'What?'

'They're telepathic. Drander thinks they can communicate all across the universe, not just locally.'

'Oh, wow.'

I'd forgotten my two worlds at camp—work and leisure—never intersected. My work colleagues knew everything I knew, but Bill, being one of my friends, knew almost nothing about the Aliens. So I started educating him and John. At least, that is, John half listened for a bit before drifting off again. Bill was a better audience.

Late in the afternoon, we saw the [General] walk into the hotel surrounded by his usual coterie of aides. Shortly after, a couple of Drander's people came in, one of them armed with a tagging gun.

'[No],' I said.

Naturally, they ignored me. I put John down and prepared to fight.

'What?' asked Bill.

I glared at the newcomers and ignored him. '[Don't you dare]!' I told them through gritted teeth. The one not carrying the gun tried to hold me still. I yelled, I kicked, I screamed and punched.

They yelled and punched back.

'[What is going on]?' the [General] bellowed.

I stopped and the one with the gun tried to take advantage. I snarled and ducked out of the way. '[These <swear word> want to tag us],' I said to the [General].

'My orders,' he replied matter-of-factly.

'No!' I screamed. '[I'm too far away from] Drander!' I went down on my knees, 'You can't. [The proximity thing. I need to be closer.] Please, don't.'

He blinked at me. '[You want to be back with your old master]?'

'[Yes],' I replied, not caring if I was giving him power over me, or insulting him by preferring her, I added, '[More than anything in the world],' and knew I meant it.

The [General's] eyelids dropped halfway. It was that speculative look that Drander used to get.'[Anything]?'

I remembered a similar deal years ago, and felt despair. '[Last time I agreed to that, I ended up pregnant],' I whispered. There was something on my cheeks. I brushed them with my hand and realised I was crying again.

'[I told you, we abandoned that experiment. We lost too many children. If you want to get back to your master, then you will do as I say and stay close. Understood]?'

I nodded.

The [General] switched to English. 'You will ensure these others also obey my instructions and stay close, too.'

How the hell was I supposed to do that?

I opened my mouth to protest, but Bill intervened. 'He will,' he said.

I felt giddy with relief.

The [General] waved the taggers out. 'You are free to move around the building, but only this building. You will not leave it without my permission. You will eat where and when we do. And you WILL eat.'

I nodded again.

He left, leaving the door open. I collapsed against the bed. I closed my eyes, and realised I was still crying.

'Care to explain?' Bill asked gently after a few minutes.

I didn't, but he needed to know what had just happened. I explained how most tags were geared to a specific person, your "master", and that, unless something special was done by your master, you couldn't stray more than a certain distance from them. Drander was my "master". Drander was still a long way away. Which meant any tag I got here would be geared to the [General]. If I was going to wear a tag, I wanted to wear it for her, not him. I got a bit stuck trying to explain why I felt so strongly about that, but Bill patted my shoulder and seemed to understand. I stopped trying to put into words something I understood less than he seemed to.

When I felt calm enough again, I picked John up and we went hunting for the kitchens and more linen and toothbrushes and other necessities.

It was like the bad old times all over again, except that now there was more than one of me, the Aides thought twice about picking on us. Besides they seemed to think John was cute and vied with each other to pay attention to him. He very quickly got over his fear of them and started enjoying it. I had to intervene when one of them tried to give him some of that yellow wobbly stuff, but I figured a little spoiling wouldn't hurt him and let them.

Occasionally someone would order us back to our room, and Bill and I would collect him and despite his protests, drag him up with us.

One afternoon we were in our room in time to see a truck unload a batch of Humans. There was no sign of them when we went downstairs for tea later.

Bill pushed his food around on his plate until the [General] noticed and ordered him to eat. He looked mutinous, but I managed to catch Bill's eye and hope he understood the plea in mine. He glared at us both, but obediently took a mouthful and chewed.

Back in our room he refused to speak with me.

It hurt.

I was surprised at how much it hurt. I couldn't remember a time when I hadn't been surrounded by people who hated me, including myself. But Bill was somehow different. I cared about what Bill thought of me.

But what could I do? I could hardly stop what was happening. Us Humans were conducting a guerrilla war against the invaders, and it was their job to stop us. How did what the [General] was doing differ from what I had done when I had annihilated a thousand hatchlings?

I left Bill with John and went for a walk. Not being allowed to leave the building, I headed for the roof. Had I become some sort of inhuman monster that I couldn't care like Bill did? Did that make me a psychopath?

I suddenly remembered a law lecturer explaining the legal difference between a sociopath and a psychopath.

And then I remembered why John couldn't be my son. I remembered Patricia leaving me before he was born. Except, in the camp, they had called her "Trish", where I had called her "Patsy" when we were married; and she had called me Jack. Only I wasn't Jack.

My brother and I were John and Josh. I was older by two minutes, but he was brainier and a better athlete, and had glorious black curls to my straight black hair. We were the youngest of four.

The memories came flooding back, raw, unfiltered, unwelcome. With both parents being judges, we four children spent a lot of time together, largely unsupervised. I remembered our eldest brother dying, watching as he fell headfirst off our roof after climbing up to rescue our sister Rachel's kite. Then Rachel, tucked out of sight in an institution after failing to commit suicide. And I remembered Josh. Josh finally admitting to our very straight Catholic parents that he was gay, and the disgrace that it entailed. The painful interview with my father, the High Court Judge, saying the family honour was now all on me. I was now their only child, and it was my duty to carry on the family name.

And then I found out I couldn't.

I never told them why. Just walked out on them. On them; on my promising law degree; on my whole life.

And I took a new name and made a new life far away from them and everything I had known. A life where my skills at arguing whether someone was a sociopath, or a psychopath didn't mean the difference between a jail sentence or indefinite incarceration in a place like the one Rachel was stuck in.

As I sat on that cold dark roof, reeling at each new revelation, I realised something else. Patsy and I had never really loved each other. We were a mutual convenience to each other. "Friends with benefits" like Michelle. Was I even capable of love? And I was back to that question which had started everything.

One of the [General's people] came out onto the roof beside me, and I moved aside to make room for him. If he wanted to thump me or harass me there was nothing I could do to stop him, but there was no need to attract that sort of attention by being in his way. I huddled into myself, head on my knees, and returned to my anguished thoughts.

When my new companion just stood there making no move to use the space I'd made, I lifted my head and looked at him. The [General] himself was looking at me with that double eyelid look.

My heart sank.

'[Your friend is unhappy with us].'

Actually, he didn't use the word "friend". That concept was alien to them, but I knew he meant Bill. '[We saw some Humans arrive earlier today].'

'Aah.' Even when said by an Alien, this single sound still held the usual connotations.

'What happened to them?'

The [General] twitched his ears. '[Dead. Shot. Probably].'

'[If you are going to shoot them, why bring them here]?'

'[Information of course. They are <something> fighters. We need what we can get from them].'

I tasted bile and resisted the urge to spit. 'Why not me?'

'[You]?'

'[Yes. Bill says I'm some kind of] pet [to you].'

'Pet?'

I explained what a pet was.

He blew a raspberry. '[Do these creatures answer back and tell me I am doing the wrong thing? Do they attack their masters]?'

'[Abuse them enough, they will. And I don't attack you. Or answer back].'

'[Your friend wanted to].'

'[He doesn't like what you are doing to the Humans].' '[What did he expect? We are at war].'

'[I know].' I sighed. '[Why do you treat us differently]?'

He started to answer, then stopped. Tried again, but bit that back too. Then finished lamely by saying, 'Drander wants you back.'

Was it possible he was genuinely fond of me? Or Drander? Had I heard him correctly? 'I want her back too,' I told him.

'[And for some reason our other half have asked that we comply],' the [General] added.

'[Other half]?'

'[What you and Drander call 'the ship people'].
They want you back with her too.'

Other half? Those skeletal creatures from the ships? They were the male to the [General]'s female? Or the other way around, or whatever. I hadn't thought of that relationship when Brett and I were trying to sort out the Aliens. They were so unlike each other.

'[They told you where I was]?' I hoped that wasn't it. That would be a betrayal, and I trusted them. I needed to trust in their neutrality. It was the one stable point in this whole mess.

'[No. You Humans "rescued" some failed experiments. You removed the tags and threw most of them out in transit, but someone hung onto one. We just followed the trail].'

I groaned. *What idiot had tried to souvenir something like that?*

'[Exactly].' He nodded.

'[Is that why you don't question me and] Bill? [Because the ship people have an interest in me]?'

'[Would you talk]?'

'[Probably not].'

'[Then there's no point, is there]?'

I dropped my single eyelid halfway looking up at him, still in the doorway. I wondered how long I would really hold out if they got serious. I had worked in Intelligence; I knew things they didn't. Things they were unlikely to get out of anyone else. Things they were probably willing to kill many Humans to get.

He blew soft raspberries at me. '[You forget we had you for over two of your years. If you were going to talk you would have. I know you know things we want, but I know you will die before you betray your people].'

I blinked in surprise.

The raspberries grew louder. '[Not once during our experiments did you give us the source of your information about the hatchlings. Not once did you offer me a deal to save yourself. Rather the opposite, in fact, if you remember].'

I did. And blinked some more. I may not have loved any Human woman, but I wasn't a monster. I *was* capable of love. As I thought of Drander and Chef and the others I knew that with absolute certainty. This war with the Aliens may have hardened me to some things, it may have turned me into a killer, but it hadn't completely destroyed me.

I stood up and the [General] ushered me back inside, closing and locking the door behind us.

So, no more sojourns to the roof. He must have come looking specifically for me. Which told me a lot.

The room was dark when I returned. From the snuffling sounds in the bed I could tell that the still-healing John was asleep, but Bill, in his blanket on the floor, was silent. That meant he was awake. I squatted beside him. He rolled over and turned his back. My heart contracted again, and I went into the bathroom to wash away a fresh onslaught of tears.

I slept in and caused us to be late for breakfast.

The [General] signalled one of Drander's people and pointed to Bill. I pushed him out of the way and faced the [General]. 'It's my fault.'

'You know how the system works. Either him or the hatchling.'

I swore at him.

Unfortunately, in my anger, I forgot which language I was using and the only people in the room who didn't understand me were Bill and John. The [General] had been very indulgent with me, but this was something he couldn't ignore. He gave me a back handed swipe that sent me hurtling into an ornate marble fireplace. I heard the crack as my head hit something. I have no recollection what.

I tried opening my eyes, but the penetrating light was so painful. I think I groaned because someone tugged on my hand. I opened my eyes a fraction and tried to see who. But they wouldn't focus on anything. Moving my head even minutely made things worse.

'[You're awake].'

I tried again and managed to bring the [General] into a blurry sort of focus. I shut my eyes again. 'I don't suppose you could see your way clear to give me a bit of help?'

'What do you think?'

I guessed that was a "no". 'What I did was unforgiveable, I know. You want a public apology?'

'More.'

More? What *more*? I opened my eyes again, this time noticing John's tear blotched face inches from mine. I tried to smile reassuringly at him, but this just produced fresh tears. I sighed and concentrated on the [General] again. 'What?'

'You worked in Intelligence.'

How the hell did he know that? 'If you know that then you already have an informer.'

'[The hatchling let it slip]. You didn't tell me.'

'There's not much to tell. I was writing a dictionary for them. That's all.'

'What is your leader's name?'

I almost wept with relief. 'I don't know. We used a nickname for him. I never saw or heard his name.'

'Describe him.'

That I could do. Except I couldn't. Odds were he was dead in all the rubble that was once our base, but he would have been their first priority to get to safety, so he may have got away. I tried to shake my head but that sent stars dancing and rockets shooting through my head.

'Who was your supervisor?'

He was probably dead too. They were all probably dead. But, as I thought about that gentle man with the brilliant mind and the dancing earrings so like Josh's, I found I couldn't say anything.

'Your colleagues' names and descriptions?'

Brett and Fiona and Sung and Ali. I called up a mental image of each of them in turn; and kept silent.

'I can alleviate your pain.'

I tried to focus on him again. 'I'll live. Or not.'

All up to him at this point in time.

John tugged my hand again.

The [General] came closer and loomed over me. 'Drander.'

'Don't. Please don't,' I whispered.

'You know how the system works,' he said.

Yes, I knew.

I whimpered and screwed my eyes up against yet another onslaught of tears. But then a strange calmness came over me. I thought of Drander going out every night with food for the refugees, allowing me to harbour a known fugitive, owning a jacket which was perfect for clandestine nocturnal activities, collaborating with her brother in the mass killings of their babies to thwart her masters; and I knew what she would want me to do.

I forced myself to look up at him. 'Tell her I'm sorry.'

He swam out of focus again, and I closed my eyes with a sigh. Even he could do no worse to me now.

He leant over me and held my chin in his great hand and said, 'Open.'

Surprised, I did as asked and received the globule. I blinked at him, already feeling its healing properties flowing through me. 'But—'

'As we discussed last night, you are not one of the ones who will talk. There are other things I need to spend my time on.'

'How grovelling do you want the public apology?' My way of saying thanks.

He almost smiled. 'Be ready to leave an hour after breakfast. You are confined to quarters till then.'

With my head aching the way it did, that suited me fine. 'I'll be okay,' I said to John. 'A bit sore for a couple of days, but I will heal.'

He smiled tremulously at me. I closed my eyes and retreated from the pain.

'Ow!'

I opened my eyes and saw Bill standing by the open door, rubbing his nose. I blew raspberries, remembering a similar occasion years ago, when I had tried to walk through an invisible barrier.

'How?' Bill asked.

'I don't know. Drander could do it too.'

'She locked you in?'

'Confined me to the hotel for a bit. I convinced her to drop it later the same day.'

He came over to the bed and sat just below my hip level, hunched over, not looking at me. I looked at him, and just knew the waiter had carried out the [General]'s order.

I reached for his hand. 'I'm sorry, Bill.'

'It's not your fault.'

Actually, it was, but I wasn't going to argue with him. He sat there, chewing his bottom lip.

'Ale, how long were you with them?'

'They sent Drander to us on Day One of the Invasion.'

'And you ... you've been coping with ... with this ...' Unconsciously he twisted his hand in a very familiar gesture and I flinched. He sighed and looked me fully in the face. 'People kept telling Roger and me that you were crazy. It's a bloody miracle you're as sane as you are. How did you manage?'

'When Drander first came to us, she didn't know any other way of treating people. She learnt quickly. The [General] was a bit slower, but he learnt too.' Bill opened his mouth, but I continued. 'I know you think otherwise, but he has been incredibly forbearing with me. That might change now I've overstepped the mark, but he has been gentle and considerate up to now. And his interest in me has stopped his aides from doing too much damage. I've been quite lucky, really.'

Until now.

'Lucky?? You call this lucky?'

I did.

'God help the unlucky ones, then.'

Indeed. As I had already said to Bill, sometimes it was better to be among the dead. 'Why were you trying to leave anyway?'

Bill gestured to John, curled up under my armpit. 'He needs medical attention again.'

'Just yell. Word will get passed around, and someone will come to see what the ruckus is. They don't like noise.'

Looking dubious, he yelled. He turned around and leant against the force field. It looked so ludicrous, him leaning against nothing like that, that I blew raspberries. He realised what I was laughing at and reluctantly joined in.

The Medical staff, when they came, clucked over John, and tried to take him with them. The force field, which had let them in, would not let them pass with him in tow. Nor would Bill, but it was obvious that the thought of fighting them now terrified him. I still hurt too much to care.

They fetched the [General]. He was not happy and rumbled at them. One of them prostrated themselves and spoke. It was all medical technical jargon and my head hurt too much to try to work it out. I tried to tune it out but found the [General] looking at me with concern. He cut short the doctor and pointed at me. '[Examine].' The doctor had the gall to protest. The [General] stared him down. '[I need them all fit to travel].'

They shone lights in my eyes, which still hurt, and ran surprisingly gentle fingers over a lump on my forehead. They shook their head. '[Two or three days. Not tomorrow].'

'[They go to the ship tomorrow].'

'[Then ask the ship to drop the <something>. We need to take the child to our <something else>].'

The first word had to be related to the force field, and I guessed "surgery" for the second. At least I hoped that's what it meant. The [General] nodded and spoke into his phone.

Bill gave a startled yelp and fell backwards out of the room. The [General] blew raspberries as he reached out and pulled him back in. Embarrassed, Bill sidled into another corner of the room, still trying to stay out of the way; not an easy task given how crowded our room had become.

'[You can heal them both]?'

'[The child, yes. We have his DNA. But you are the one who is compatible with the big Human. You need to treat him. Try hourly treatments until nightfall. We'll examine him again when we bring the child back].'

The [General] growled and came over to the bed. '[Open],' he ordered.

I wasn't sure I wanted anyone this annoyed administering to me. On the other hand, I didn't want to annoy him any further. I did what I was told. This wasn't a time to engage in heroics. The doctors picked up John again and headed for the door. With the [General] there, Bill only raised a token protest.

'What are they going to do, Ale?'

'Hopefully, heal him. They've taken him to a hospital or something. It's okay. They are going to bring him back.'

'Sure?'

'That's what they told the [General]. No-one lies to the [General].'

'That, I can understand,' he muttered. He slid to the floor and squatted on his haunches.

I felt well enough now to prop myself up and address him. 'Bill, I won't pretend it's alright, or even that it won't happen again. But it's over. They don't bear grudges. They have moved on. They will expect you to do that too.'

He sighed and stared at the floor. 'I ... I ...' He shook his head. 'I've never felt pain like it before. I thought I was going to die. I couldn't breathe. I ... I panicked. I think I blacked out too.'

'Ouch. That was nasty. He pushed the blood out of your heart. Drander has only ever done that once, but then she nursed my body to normalcy. There was no need to do anything so extreme just because we were late for breakfast.'

'Um.' He flushed. 'That isn't why they did it. I yelled at Crocodile Face for hurting you.'

I blew a short raspberry. It hurt. 'He had a real good morning of it, didn't he? Both his little pets turned on him.'

Bill opened his mouth, then saw the humour of it. He grinned reluctantly. 'I think I know how you've survived.'

'Oh?'

'You can see their point of view. And you've got a great sense of humour. Not to mention enough resilience for a dozen men.'

'You'll give me a swollen head.'

'Don't worry. I'll find some way to shrink it back again.'

That was my Bill. He was no stranger to humour and resilience either. I lay back down and wondered where my so-called resilience had been when I found out I was to be my parents' ultimate disappointment. Every one of their children had failed them, and there weren't going to be any grandchildren. Well, there were worse things in life. I thought about my family of Drander, and the five, now six children, who would become a significant part of my life when I got back home. They didn't need to be my flesh and blood for me to care about them.

An hour later I was woken by the [General], but apart from commenting that I must have been having a pleasant dream, he didn't stay. I was just one of many tasks that he had to achieve in the hour and he was going about it as efficiently as possible, as always.

Just like the two judges who happened to be my parents. Having drawn that corollary, I also began to recognise others, and to understand our relationship. As the third of four children of high-powered busy parents, and not the brightest, or the greatest achiever, or the only girl, or having any other distinguishing specialities, my parents had unwittingly prepared me to stand up for myself and rely on no-one to get what I needed out of life. The [General] had no patience for terrified sycophants. He wanted to be surrounded by people who could look him in the eye and calmly and succinctly state their case. So, until this morning, that is what I'd been giving him. My irreverent larrikin Australian sense of humour, and innate belief that all people are born equal, had also been helping me to cope. It enabled me to see Drander and the [General] and the people from the ship as—well, not Human Beings exactly—but certainly no better or worse.

Satisfied I'd solved all life's mysteries, I fell asleep again. Only to be woken by the [General] again.

'Why am I so tired?' I complained to Bill as I struggled to keep my eyes open after he left.

'Because your body has gone into super healing mode.'

'Huh?'

Bill sat beside me again and touched my forehead. 'I can see it, Ale. It's happening in front of my eyes. I've never seen a crack like that heal so fast. Can you focus, yet?'

I could. It wasn't painful either. Something else was, though.

'I'm starving.'

'Probably.'

'What?' That wasn't the normal reaction to a statement like that.

'Told you—super healing mode. You need lots and lots of fuel and rest to sustain it.'

I yawned, and forced my eyes open again. 'Ask for food.'

He bit his lips and looked away from me. It was obvious I'd have to do it myself. That must have been one hell of an experience this morning to make him like this. I'd have to help him. Later. When I was awake. I drifted off again.

I woke up attached to the familiar catheter and drip. Automatically my hands went to my mouth and I checked my lips and was absurdly pleased to find no stitches, even as my brain caught up with the fact that they didn't do "that" any longer.

Bill chuckled.

I rolled over and looked askance at him.

'He said you'd do that. Lay me odds on it.'

I smiled. 'What did you lose?'

He shook his head. 'I was there when you arrived. Remember?'

I remembered. 'I take it you didn't accept his bet, then?'

Bill shook his head again and held up a piece of purple stuff. 'Hungry? He finally consented to feed us. Journey rations, I think. It's tough and chewy.'

I didn't care, I was still famished. The shadow looked wrong on my hand as I reached out. 'What time is it?'

'Almost tea time. You've been out like a light for about six hours. He called the medics when you didn't rouse the third time. That was about five visits ago.'

I chewed the unpalatable stuff, wondering. 'He didn't say anything about what we're doing tomorrow or why, did he?'

'Not that I understood. Why?'

I sighed. 'He said we're "going to the ship tomorrow", and I don't know what he meant by it.'

Bill shrugged, 'Guess we'll find out.'

They returned John to us about midnight, looking much better, but at the uncomfortable stage of healing—neither well enough to do anything yet nor sick enough to do nothing. About the same time, I finally felt well enough to try to drag myself and my drip across the room. Bill was so busy caring for both of us, he forgot to be frightened when the [General] wandered back in for the final check-up of the night.

'Breakfast will be delivered. Be ready to leave one of your hours after,' he told us as he left.

None of us slept—John and I were too uncomfortable, and Bill was too concerned about us—and we had nothing to pack except toothbrushes pilfered from the hotel's stores. So, we were actually ready before the long night was over and breakfast finally arrived.

One of the [General]'s aides came for us. I was so weak still that he lost patience and slung me over his shoulder in a fireman's lift and dumped me at the [General]'s feet on the road in front of the hotel. The [General] leant down and helped me back to my feet. I could have sworn he was trying NOT to blow raspberries. I bowed to hide my embarrassment.

'[Good Morning, Human].'

I solemnly returned the greeting. Risked a glance up at him. He was definitely trying not to laugh. I sighed. 'Go on,' I said.

'About that apology?' he asked instead.

I tilted my head up so I was looking him in the eye, or as much as was possible from our different heights. 'I did say I would, didn't I?'

He nodded solemnly.

I thought about it. 'Can we do it some other time? I'm not sure I'm capable of getting back up again if I kneel down.'

An eyelid fluttered. That was a new one. I had no idea what that meant. '[Apologise].'

Clutching my drip for support, I got down on my knees, and then prostrated myself. '[I did wrong. Forgive].' And waited for what seemed like an eternity.

Then he reached down and gently lifted me up until I was eye to eye with him. 'Next time do it in your own language.'

'I'm sorry. I forget which is which.'

He blinked in surprise. And gave in to the laugh which had been trying to escape. '[Go],' he said, pointing to a troop carrier. '[In the back. All three of you].'

Needless to say, I needed help getting in. But once in, the others in the carrier, mostly Drander's people, allowed us to sit, and mostly left us alone for the hour-long journey to one of the ships.

Bill jumped out when we got there and lifted John down. While he was doing that [the ship people] came out and flew over to me. It was them who picked me up and flew me to the ground.

One of them touched my forehead and uttered a roar. I blinked at him, and then blinked some more when every Alien in our vicinity fled.

'[What]?' I chittered in their language.

'[Who]?' It stroked my forehead again.

'[The General. I swore at him. He punished me].'

Raspberries repeated across the open field between the ship and the carrier by the many [ship people] who had come pouring out. I'd never seen more than four before. But hundreds seem to have answered the roar. I had no idea there were so many.

'Heeero,' the one directly in front of me whispered.

My head still hurt, and I was exhausted from lack of sleep and trying to super heal. I just nodded when it said that and slumped against the carrier.

'[Open].'

'[The General has been doing that].'

More raspberries, and some energetic chittering. I got the hint and opened. The headache instantly vanished, and I felt energised enough to stand up again. The [General]'s saliva was good, but these guys' was much better. I bowed my thanks to it.

The [General] rounded the corner of the carrier escorted by multiple [ship people] at various heights around him. He didn't look happy. 'What is going on?' he asked me.

I shook my head. 'You tell me. I have no idea.'

'[Ship],' a hundred voices said to us.

Bill, John, and I were flown across the intervening space and taken up into the ship, but the [General] had to walk.

Inside the ship, the light was so dim I couldn't make out much, except that we were in a large cavernous area. Boxes of the sort I used to take delivery of were stacked to one side of a moving walkway. Rows of reclining seats moved into the distance on the other side. It was the walkway we were deposited on. By the time the [General]'s bulk blocked the light in the hatchway, we were already a long way from the entrance.

Then we moved upwards. Bill and I both grabbed for John when the square we were standing on started its ascent.

'[The child is quite safe],' we were told.

'[He's barely out of hatchling stage].'

'[He cannot fall].'

I had my doubts about that, but I had never known them be wrong before, so I reluctantly let go. I needn't have worried. John was so awed by what was happening, he seemed incapable of moving anyway.

The next level was a maze of corridors through which our square and escort of hovering [ship people] took us. Eventually we stopped outside a large window overlooking a room filled with junior versions of the [General]'s people.

It was here the [General] caught up with us. '[You can't].' He seemed to be pleading with our hosts.

They opened their eyes fully and stared him down.

In the dim light of the ship, which I was gradually adjusting to, their inner eyelid no longer covered their eyes, giving a luminescent sheen to their eyes.

'[Tell them why you stopped the experiment],' they ordered him.

He heaved a huge sigh. And then another.

I tore my eyes away from the children and looked at him, concerned. '[General]?'

He was watching one child in particular. Taller and slimmer than the others, he was on his own, building a tower of blocks. The other "boys" were mostly in groups, wrestling, kicking balls, or doing other group type physical activities. But not this boy.

I had a sudden revelation. 'Ours?' I asked.

'[Yes].'

A pause, then the [General] said, '[I had hoped to foster him with you].'

I watched the child for a while. He was as tall as John, and easily as co-ordinated. And bright. He already knew to start his block tower with a pyramid like base. It was hard to believe he was only half John's age.

'I'd be delighted to have him,' I said sincerely.

'All the Human-carried children turn. That's really why we stopped. Your second child turned so fast we barely made it to the ship with him.'

'Turned?'

He sighed. 'All children are born like this,' he said, pointing to his own chest. 'Some [turn]. Become like that.' He pointed to a hovering [ship person]. '[Ship people] cannot survive outside the ship except in space. We cannot survive in space. We need an atmosphere and light. We like our food—they do not eat food.'

I looked at the child again. 'All except ours.'

'He has not turned, because he knows I do not want him to turn.' There was something wrong with the

[General]'s voice, and I looked up at him, and realised his eyes were lined with luminescent tears.

'[If he turns, he cannot leave the ship. He cannot live with you. Can never be a great General like me].'

I reached up and took one of his great hands in mine. 'What is best for him?'

The [General] turned away from me. 'I had no idea you were so important to them. I hurt you. My punishment is to give up my child. Allow him to turn.'

'[I insulted you. I told them it was my fault].'

'Heero,' one of them said.

'[He cannot survive in his current form. He is not strong],' another said.

'[You must allow the change],' said yet another.

The [General] leant his head against the window. Several children looked up at the bulk looking in on them, including our child. A broad smile, and he left his blocks to come over to us.

On the way, one of the boys from a group tripped him up. He twisted almost in mid-air and kicked out at them. His long legs connected, but there was no strength in them, and they just laughed and shoved him back down.

'[Allow the change. Now].' A ship person ordered.

The [General] thumped the glass with his other hand and bellowed. Everyone inside the room stopped what they were doing and looked. '[Tell him],' he whispered slumping against the glass.

And then a miracle happened.

The boy lying on the ground grew pale and seemed to stretch. He roared and rose into the air. The boys who had been teasing him backed away. Our child roared again, and they fell. I could not see how.

His wings unfurled, and he rose higher. I now saw that the nursery had no roof, and he came gliding over the partition towards us. He was less than half the size of the adults hovering around us, but they greeted him as an equal. Landing next to us, he greeted his "father" and then looked at me. 'Hero,' he whispered and held out his hand.

I took it with my free hand and gently shook. Despite his youth and size, it was clear he was already part of the gestalt and knew all about me.

I could see how the [General] would consider that he had just lost his child, but I felt honoured to have carried one, no two, of [the ship people] to birth. I looked down on my child with pride and love in my heart and considered that he was so young to have had such a massive transformation thrust upon him, not just physically, but mentally.

I let go of the [General] and knelt and hugged my child, knowing as I did so that I was hugging all the [ship people] all over the galaxy and maybe beyond, but thinking only to comfort a frightened child who must surely be confused and in pain.

He returned the hug with all the strength that frail little body had, and from hundreds of throats I heard 'Hero' whispered.

Then the child looked me in the eye and said, 'Thank you,' quite clearly.

Looking beyond me to the [General], he added, '[Call our people back. We are leaving this planet].'

The [General] looked as though he would argue the point. I stood up and faced him, my hands still on our child's shoulders and opened my eyes as wide as they would go.

Bill told me afterwards that as I straightened up and stared the [General] down, [the ship people] had surrounded me, above and beside me, so that it looked like I was standing in the midst of a horde of angry wasps.

The [General] closed his mouth, sucked his lips in, and inclined his head. '[I will start the <something> process].'

I have no idea where we were, but it was only about five minutes later that the hatchway reopened onto a familiar park. I almost bolted down the hatchway, remembering at the last minute to turn and thank our hosts. They blew raspberries at me and told me to go. I needed no further prompting; I left it to Bill to follow with John and ran.

A tall, slim, and very pretty girl with fair hair was vacuuming the restaurant as I entered. She switched off the vacuum and asked if she could help me, but then she stopped, looking puzzled.

'Hi, Rita,' I said, 'Drander about?'

Her jaw dropped. 'Uncle Ale?' she whispered, and then shouted, 'It's Uncle Ale. Uncle Ale's back!' And she came running and threw her arms around me. Suddenly I was surrounded by people, real Human people, all of whom seemed to want to hug me or shake my hands. I'm sure Enya even kissed me.

Then, at the back of the crowd, holding a dark-haired Asian boy on her hip, stood a Human sized green Alien with large velvety eyes brimming with a luminescent rim. The crowd just fell away as I walked forward. And suddenly I was trembling and there were tears in my eyes too. I couldn't speak. I couldn't breathe. Someone took Robin from her and we faced each other less than two inches apart.

She sucked her lips in and a tear slid down her cheek. I reached out and wiped it away and then she was in my arms and we were kissing and crying each other's names, and I was babbling in her tongue and she was babbling in mine. And then we stopped, and just looked into each other's eyes.

'I love you,' I whispered with a voice gone suddenly gruff.

She nodded, and we kissed full on the lips, and if the nose on my face ever bothered her, she never ever let on.

On his last day, the [General] came to visit us. He looked tired, and I sat him down at an empty table. Our little restaurant was a bit crowded these days. It was now home to Bill's clinic, and the locals had also started to return as word of my—ahem—heroism in the lion's den was spreading. Bill can be eloquent when he wants to be. According to him, it was my actions on the ship which single-handedly caused the Aliens' retreat.

Anyway, I found a rare empty table, and while Drander made the coffee, I went down to the cellar and brought up my last bottle of Federation Port. We'd used the previous bottle on my first night back, to drink to the end of the War, my safe return, and Robin saying his first words in three years, and well ... just because we wanted to.

The [General] rolled it around his tongue in appreciation. '[You never offered us this before],' he said.

'[Very expensive. Impossible to replace],' I told him with a smile. '[The bottle is yours. Take it with you].'

He blinked. 'Thank you.'

He sipped some more, and asked, '[What happened]?'

'[You got outmanoeuvred],' Drander said.

He tilted his head.

'[The ship people need you. They need you to fertilise their eggs. You need planetfall, so they periodically drop you off and wait around until you are ready to leave, but they usually pay no attention to what you are actually doing, do they]?' I asked.

He nodded. '[Until now].'

'[You need us].' Drander took up the tale, sitting beside me, holding my hand. '[You need us to carry the fertilised egg. We exist to nurture and care for your young and your sick. And they need us. They cannot eat without our assistance. But on the last trip the ship people realised you were changing us, warping us to do your dirty work, breeding armies of us with the sole purpose of hurting people].'

I took up the explanation again. '[They didn't approve. They did some of their own breeding. Drander and her batchlings are from one of their batches. They infiltrated their carers amongst yours. Someone worked out some of them had missed tagging and tagged them. After that what Drander and Dr'gor could do was somewhat limited. Then I happened. I wasn't tagged. I could go where they couldn't. And you were breeding armies again].'

He sipped and nodded sagely, that is with two eyelids half down.

'[And then he confounded them by teaching them manners],' Drander said.

The [General] blinked.

I blushed. This bit embarrassed me. I hadn't thought it at all odd. '[I said] thank you [to them, when they helped me].'

'Thank you?'

I nodded.

Drander continued, '[They were already paying more attention than normal to your activities, but after that they started paying attention to the local inhabitants, especially Ale. They lost him when you took him in to be a carrier. When they found him again, he was almost at death's door. They passed the message on about his location to someone with contacts to the resistance].'

The [General] blinked really rapidly.

'[I got rescued. Then they lost me again when the camp moved. The ship person sent to find me allowed itself to be captured].'

'[And then he confounded them again, by defying his own people and rescuing it],' Drander continued.

'[And then you bombed our camp. I'm pretty sure that was when they really decided enough was enough—not later when I met our child. He sends his] love [by the way].'

'[What]?'

'[I see him whenever his ship is in the park. Who do you think told me all this]?'

The [General]'s ears twitched, but he also shrugged his shoulders. The next generation were either going to be really confused or bilingual—or both.

I leant forward and took the [General]'s huge hand in mine. '[We haven't lost him. When you speak to any ship person, you are speaking to them all. Even if it is not him physically, he is aware of you. They all are. They've stopped calling me] Hero [now. They all call me] Mother. [He calls you] Father. And he still loves you.

'[He also has another message for you],' I told him as we farewelled him. '[He knew that you would drop in and say goodbye before you left, and he asked that this be the last thing we said, before you go to the ship].'

The [General] tilted his head.

Drander took my hand, and said, '[It is never too late to turn].'

The eyes blinked, and the jaw dropped, but then the eyelids steadied at the halfway point and he sucked in his lips.

'Thank you.' He took a deep breath. 'Thank you so much.'

And he almost ran from us.

Ship people do not eat. They can't, they have no stomach. The space required is taken up by the muscles needed to manage their wings. Nutrition is pumped directly into the blood stream by the carers. I like to think that the last thing he had "by mouth" was my Federation Port.

Printed in June 2019
by Rotomail Italia S.p.A., Vignate (MI) - Italy